PLATINUM TIES

II

Summer's Heat

By, G. Barrett-Jones

This is a work of fiction. Names, characters, and incidents are either the product of the author's imagination or are used fictitiously, and any resemblance to actual people, living or dead is entirely coincidental.

Hearts…Two, three or more
Tied together as one
Stronger than platinum
Love has no equal…
It is a fire never quenched and a life neither death nor the
grave can conquer.

BACK DOWN MEMORY LANE

The clock read ten thirty but it felt much later. Martie had been gazing at a photo of a beautiful young Gertie Mae for at least thirty minutes. The picture was dated March 16, 1938. Gertie Mae was twenty-one-years-old—a real fox. Judging by those gorgeous eyes, full lips, and hanging earrings, no one would think of the hell that woman had come through. She didn't look like a mother of a little girl, whose father was either Gertie Mae's father, uncle, or cousin. They all had their turn. Gertie Mae's mom died when she was twelve, leaving her to become the woman of the house. It was more like being a slave or somebody's dog—or less—especially after the natural love of a father was only expressed in his bedroom. Uncle Herbert, her father's brother was next in line, and finally, Uncle Herbert's son, cousin Wilfred had his share of her too. Gertie Mae was fourteen when she ran away from the hellhole, only to discover she was pregnant by one of those dirty bastards. Apart from domestic duties and satisfying needs, Gertie Mae knew next to nothing, and certainly nothing about rearing a child. But one thing she did know, was that she would never go back to Marksville, Louisiana, and she never did. Martie smiled, thinking about how much she and Gertie

Mae had in common. Even though her dad had never touched her in such a horrible way, someone else did. Her dad died before she was born, and from the things she had heard about him, she knew he would have never done such a thing. However, Martie was five years old when her mom married a devil named Larry Broussard, who had patiently watched Martie from the day he and his son, Larry Jr. moved in. Martie vividly recalled the day she became the victim of Larry Broussard's lust. It was on a Sunday afternoon. Dark clouds had just begun to roll in and the smell of rain was in the air. Louise was busy at the church while the devil was busy at her home. Martie was just a precious lamb of ten years old on that day. As Martie's mind drifted further into the laborious journey of memories, the pungent odor of a disturbed ant bed on a hot summer day filled her nostrils, and the phone rang. Martie quickly answered, faking agitation because it was three o'clock in the morning. But when Martie heard Gertie Mae's voice on the other end of the line, a huge smile came over her face.

"Woman, you are going to live a long time. I was just thinking about you."
Gertie Mae replied that she had been thinking about her too, which is why she called. She said she

couldn't rest in peace until she talked with her. She asked Martie what she'd been thinking about.

"Everything" Martie replied, "I was looking at your picture, and my mind just drifted. I thought about when Louise sent me to Ville Platte to Ms. Hattie's and I called you, and you came and got me. You saved my baby's life."

Gertie Mae chuckled. "I rememba. It was Decemba fifteen…and it was freezing dat day. I was leavin da house an I start not tuh ansuh dat phone. But I'm glad I did."
Martie freely talked, running off at the mouth, describing her vivid memories as if she was watching her 15-year-old self on a television screen. She could see herself and Lousie at the Greyhound Bus station; it was three o'clock in the morning. Louise was fussing at her and promising there was no way she was going raise two children in her home. Martie knew Louise's anger towards her wasn't about her being pregnant; it was more about being embarrassed because of what her church members would say about her having a pregnant teenage daughter. Louise taught Sunday school and was well-respected in the church. Even the children loved her, but there she was that morning, looking at her own child like she was trash.

Martie pleaded, "Mama please don't send me away…I'm sorry."

Harshly, Louise told her, "Hush you mouf I say! Nah, yere yu ticket. Hattie son, Ray, is gon meechu at duh bus place when yu get daa. And stop dat cryin. You wadn't cryin when you did this." Martie described how roughly Louise wiped Martie's tears with that balled-up napkin that she had clenched in her fist. She re-wrapped Martie's scarf and tugged and adjusted Martie's tan cashmere coat, to make sure she was presentable, and looked respectable. Martie was scared to death, and reached out to hug her mom for some comfort, but was snatched about by one arm and made to face the opened doors of the bus. Martie's feet felt like bricks. Her legs were heavy. It took all of her strength to walk up those few steps. There were only a few people were on the bus, so Martie sat in the front seat so she could see the driver and the driver could see her. The trip to Ville Platte, Louisiana from Beaumont, Texas was less than a hundred and fifty miles, but since Ville Platte didn't have a bus station, the bus stopped in Opelousas, Louisiana. It took all of nine hours to get there and Martie was famished by the time Ray pulled up in front of that old brown house with the leaning porch. Martie started crying because the house almost looked abandoned. When that big woman came out of the house dressed in a Mumu and slippers, Martie cried even harder. Ray begged her to stop crying before she made his mom think he had done something he wasn't supposed to do.

Ray quickly got out of the car explaining, "Mama, I swear I din't do dat gurl nuthin. She jus stawted cryin when I pulled up. I swear mama."
Ray opened the car door and Martie got out, still crying as she cautiously approached the porch with her arms folded, clutching her stomach. David couldn't have been much larger than an acorn, but Martie knew he was just as scared as she was. She could feel him. She swore she could feel him. But he must have been hungry too because when the smell of pork roast, greens, and cornbread hit Martie's nose, she could have run into Ms. Hattie's kitchen and eaten right out of the pots.

"Yu got da package," she asked.
Martie pulled the envelope of money from her coat and gave it to Ms. Hattie, and she opened it and flipped through the bills. Then she told Martie that Louise had told her that Martie loves roast and greens.

"I cook early so yu can eat later," she said, before inviting Martie in.

Gertie Mae sat silently on the phone while Martie talked none stop, detailing the awful bathroom, the large gown hanging on the hook behind the door, the bedroom, the bed with no sheets, the set of linens on the nightstand, the stack of towels and the three small buckets that were on the floor. There was some kind of syringe with a rubber tube and other stuff that looked like they could be used to fix things. Martie remembered being so afraid until she nearly lost her bodily functions, but that was the moment she decided she was going to keep her baby.

"And granny, for the life of me, I don't know how I remembered your number. But I picked up that phone and dialed three-three-seven-three-six-three-twenty-one, eighty-one. And I remember saying, Granny, *please* come get me! I don't know where I am, I just know her name is Ms. Hattie and Mama sent me here so she can take my baby."

"Um hum…an I say I wuz on my way, Gertie Mae replied.

"Yes ma'am…you sure did," Martie answered. Martie recalled the confrontation as she remembered hearing it, when Gertie Mae arrived at Ms. Hattie's house. She heard Ms. Hattie yell, 'Guddi Mae, nah you ain't got nuthin tuh do wit dis…that gul mama sent huh yere.' And the next thing Martie remembered hearing was a knock on the bedroom door.

"I heard your voice, saying, '*Mar-tuh…dis you granny…op da doe baby.*'
Martie described how she flung that door open so fast and ran into Gertie Mae's arms and how it felt to hear her say, 'I'm taking you home with me.' She remembered seeing Ms. Hattie standing there without saying a word as they walked past her. Martie continued, how when Louise found out what happened and how she came to Ville Platte ready to fight. That was the first time Martie had ever heard Louise cuss. Louise stood in Gertie Mae's front yard and demanded Gertie Mae send her child out of that house.

And Gertie Mae replied, "If I sen huh…yu betta keep yu hand to yusef!"

Louise put her hands on her hips and fired back, "I be *damn* if yu tell me what to do wit my own chile…and if you don't sen huh right nah, yu gon *see* what ima do to yu ass…yu old witch."
Gertie Mae walked out onto the porch with one hand on her hip and pointed her finger toward the porch,

"Yu bring yu ass yere if yu want…I bet I'll send yu ass back to whaa yu come from."

Louise started towards Gertie Mae and Gertie Mae started towards Louise.

Martie ran out of the house past Gertie Mae, screaming, "Mama Stop!"
And just like that, everybody stopping in their tracks. Even some of the neighbors who were coming to be nosey stopped. Gertie Mae was wearing a frown, but Louise was wearing a poker face. Louise was done talking and Martie knew it. Which is why Martie was keeping a good distance from Louise.

In a calm voice, like she wasn't upset at all, Louise said, "Martha Louise, getchu stuff…and les go."

Martie pleaded, "Mama, please let me keep my baby."

"Look nah." Louise gritted, "I say I'm not raisin' two churin in my house…nah getchu stuff and les go."
Martie didn't back talk, but she backed away from Louise until she reached Gertie Mae's porch. Louise just stood there and looked at Martie for a few seconds before telling Martie one more time to get her stuff. Martie didn't move.

"Den stay yu ass right whaa yu at," Louise snapped.
Louise got back into her car. She looked into the mirror to make sure her hair was in place and then

drove off without looking again in Martie's direction. On March 12, 1966, Martie felt severe cramps and passed a clot. Gertie Mae checked the clot and was sure Martie miscarried, but after a few days, Martie swore she felt little flutters now and again. A month later, after believing she had suffered a miscarriage, Martie felt her baby move, and kick, and on August 14, 1966, Gertie Mae delivered David right there in her house.

"Ooh, I thought my hips were gonna break…it felt like it was just one big hole down there," Martie recalled.

"Maa, dat chile was ten pound," Gertie Mae confirmed.

"With a big ole head huh Granny?"

"And wit eyes dat look jus like my Sylvi Ann wen she wuz bawn…I can still see him lookin round like he knowed whaa he was at," Gertie Mae recalled.

"Umm hmm…" Martie agreed, before realizing Gertie Mae had never mentioned David having eyes like her daughter Sylvia Ann, who was Larry Jr.'s mother.

A brief silence ensued, and Martie waited for Gertie Mae to say something else. When Gertie Mae did say something, she said two things Martie didn't expect to ever hear. The first of those two things was out of the question. Martie flat-out refused to give Larry Jr. the satisfaction of knowing David was his son.

"And when did you know Larry Jr. was David's daddy? I never told anybody that," Martie insisted. Gertie Mae said she knew David was Larry Jr.'s baby before he was born because Sylvia Ann came to her one night and told her that was her grandbaby Martie was carrying, and that miscarriage was not her grandbaby.

Gertie Mae said Sylvia Ann had told her some other things too— "Like how yu dint stop those richuls on that chile wen yu wuz s'posed tu." The sharpness in Gertie Mae's voice stung Martie's heart. She had never used that tone with her—ever. Martie knew she was supposed to stop the rituals on David when he reached six years old, and she did, but she did it again when David was twelve, and again when he was sixteen. She confessed, and attempted to defend her reason for it:

"I did it when he was twelve because he disobeyed me when I told him he couldn't box, and I did it another time when he was sixteen because he stopped talking to me. I couldn't have my child acting like he hated me," Martie defended.

"An wen he wuz twenty…whas yu reason fuh dat?" Gertie Mae snapped.

Embarrassed, Martie confessed what she did that last time was pure selfishness. But she did it because she was afraid David was going to marry Ara, or worse, get her pregnant. And she didn't want either, so she broke that strong attraction David had for Ara. But, to add injury to insult, Gertie Mae told Martie that the last ritual on David didn't work anyway, because he'd already become what they are, but he just hadn't realized it yet.

"An if he use dis on a woman, he gon be worse dan any man you ever know," Gertie Mae chastised. Though Martie was as guilty as a person caught in the act could be, still she hotly resisted the idea of telling Larry Jr. the truth. The second thing Gertie Mae said to her, made Martie feel like her face was going to explode. She almost cussed Gertie Mae. She swore she would rather admit to David everything she'd ever done to him before she would just hand him over to Larry Jr.

"I've been David's mama and daddy. Me, Granny! Just me!" Martie defended.
Gertie Mae's tone continued to chastise Martie and Martie kept snapping back, frustrated because she and Gertie Mae had never talked to each other with such heat. Martie felt like she was talking to Louise, which is why she couldn't back down. And when

Gertie Mae asked Martie if she loved David, Martie
answered with an emphatic,

"Yes! You know how much I love my child!"

"Den, give him to his daddy!"

"Hell no!" Martie shouted, before slamming the
phone down on the table. The loud crash jolted
Thaddeus from his sleep. He hurried into the dining
room to see what happened. Martie had knocked the
centerpiece off the table. It had crashed to the floor,
snapping Martie out of that terrible dream. She
didn't even remember falling asleep, but she hadn't
slept long. It was only ten forty-five.

AS WE LAY...

The sunlight crept in through the small opening
of the curtain and traveled across the floor. It
climbed into bed and kissed Sydney on the cheek,
but she was already awake, listening to the humming
of the air conditioner and thinking. She thought she
would feel better after getting what she wanted.
Instead, she lay there feeling terrible, like she'd made
a huge mistake, because David made her feel weak
and helpless. It wasn't supposed to happen like that.

That's not how it's supposed to be, she thought. She never feels that way with Kenny. It didn't happen that way with Terrence or De'Vonte either, she recalled. Despite being a beautiful, sunny day, with birds chirping right outside the window, it felt like it was raining. Sydney wanted to get up and run away—just get dressed and take off running. But she lay there feeling David's warm body. His chest—pressed against her back and her butt nestled against his lap. Her head rested on his right arm like a pillow, and his left hand was still clutching her stomach. He'd held on to her for most of the night, like he was afraid she would disappear. That last time he finished; he never took it out. He let it backslide naturally. That soft, *"I love you,"* that escaped his lips long after that last round, before falling asleep, was still lingering in Sydney's ear. Hearing those words from him was like putting salve on an infected cut. Although, it would have been much better if he hadn't been the one who cut her in the first place. That's why she acted like she was asleep when he said it. Sydney inhaled, and when she did, David moaned and tightened his grip—as if he could get any closer. She wondered if he was awake, or just being affectionate in his sleep, but her question was quickly answered. He was definitely awake. She felt it starting to swell against her butt, but as soon as

David tried to slide in again, Sydney squeezed and thrust away,

"No. I have to take a shower," She claimed. David snatched her back, but Sydney quickly flipped onto her back and told him again that she had to take a shower, because she was all squishy.

"Yeah, I know…just like I want it…good and marinated," David replied.

Sydney frowned and called him nasty, but when she saw that look in his eyes, that *'I'm not taking no for an answer'* look, she let him have it. He indulged and she reciprocated, and when they finished again, David relaxed and allowed the full weight of his body to rest on her. She caressed his back, but gazed at the ceiling, thinking once again about how reckless the whole ordeal had been. Not only had they gone at like rabbits throughout the night, but David was popping off rounds like he was in a western shootout. They didn't use protection. *'A fine time to think about that now,'* she thought. *'Am I trying to get pregnant,'* she wondered. *'Hell no,'* she concluded. *'Then why did I do this,'* she asked herself. *'What if I do get pregnant,'* she wondered. *'He's not even my boyfriend. I only did this to get back at Tina,'* she admitted. *'Ooh, David makes me sick,'* she concluded.

As Sydney lay there, playing in her head, she decided to verbalize some of the words from one of those letters David claimed he never received.

She whispered in his ear, "*Every night I cry at the thought of losing you twice and every morning I die from the guilt of saving my own life.*"
She waited for him to respond in a way that would tell her he knew where those words came from but he was too busy tracing her ear with his tongue and nibbling on her ear lobe.

"Sounds familiar?" Sydney asked.

"No," David replied, moving from her ear lobe to her neck.
Reality finally hit Sydney—sort of. Sydney knew David was not that cold. If he'd read those words in that letter, there was no way he would act as if he hadn't. She figured he told the truth that day when he said he never received any letters from her. Chances are, his mom never gave them to him. Suddenly, the thought of what David would think about her if he did read those letters was sickening. Her blood and guts were on those pages. Her fear and pain were there too. She aborted their baby because she was afraid. It seemed like the right thing to do back then. Writing it in a letter felt like the right thing back then, too. Now it all seemed like the worst mistake she could have made. Her mind raced,

wondering if his mom still hade those letters stashed away and if so, how she could get them back. David was kissing her again when the phone rang. It was nine-thirty in the morning. When he got up to answer the phone, Sydney hopped up too. When he answered the phone, Sydney asked for a bath towel and David shushed her.

She snapped, "Don't be shushing me for your lil girlfriend. Where's the bath towels?" she asked, intending to be heard. David motioned for her to keep her mouth shut so he could hear, but he pointed to the trunk where he kept his towels. Sydney got an attitude and flung one of the pillows at him, hitting him behind the head. Then she got in his face while he was on the phone—agitating him. Every time he moved, she moved.

She poked his sides until he took the phone away from his ear and snapped at her, "Stop!"

Surprised, by his rudeness, Sydney shoved him and walked away, loudly accusing him of acting funky with her after getting her stuff, "All night!" she yelled, intending for whoever was on the phone to know a woman spent the night with him.

David looked at her like she was crazy, before returning to his conversation, "Okay…what's up? Nah, that's just Sydney being Sydney…so, what's

wrong with her?... What?... When?... Aww, man…
Okay…okay…I'll be there," David replied.

David hung up, while Sydney was still singing in
the shower, loudly, "*What a lovely night we had…yea,
yea…as we shared each other's love. We forgot about all the
pain we caused…as we slept the night away. As we lay…*"
David stepped into the shower, looking concerned,
but Sydney smirked, thinking she must have pissed
off his caller. He didn't say anything. He just took
her washcloth, washed up quickly, rinsed, and got
out. Concerned, Sydney asked what was going on.
When David half answered, nothing, she knew
something was wrong. She stepped out of the
shower and made David look at her when she asked
again, what was wrong.

He answered, "That was Thaddeus. I gotta go
check on my mama. Granny Gertie Mae died last
night," he said.

Sydney left her car at David's and rode with him, but
he dropped her at her parent's home to wait for him
to pick her up on his way back to Liberty. It was
twelve-thirty when David arrived at his mom's
house, with sandwiches from Tillman's bar-b-que—
two links and one chopped beef sandwich. He
bought the chopped beef for Thaddeus just in case
he was hungry. He didn't buy his mom anything
because he knew she would only ask for a bite of his

sandwich. David rang the doorbell instead of using his key, and Thaddeus opened the door with his finger covering his mouth, suggesting David remain quiet.

"Your mom has been crying all morning," He whispered.

David handed Thaddeus his bar-b-que sandwich and walked into the thick sadness filling Martie's room. She was sitting on the bed with her back against the headboard—legs crossed and looking dazed. She looked at David as if she was wondering who he was. No smile. No greeting. No facial expression—just a red nose, glossy eyes, and a blank stare.

When David walked over and kissed her forehead, she forced a smile. "Hey handsome," she whispered. "Tillman's?"

"Yep," David answered, and sat next to her.

"Smells good. Link?" Martie asked.

"Yep."

"Can I have a bite?"

"Sure."

Thaddeus was standing in the bedroom doorway chewing and Martie asked Thaddeus what he had. "Chopped beef. Want a bite?" He asked.

Martie frowned and shook her head, no. And then with an extremely delayed reaction, she asked David why he rang the doorbell instead of using his key.

"Because I didn't want to catch you witcho legs all up in the air," he claimed.

"Hmph. You ain't gon catch me with me with my legs all up in the air. You might catch Thaddeus with his legs up in the air," Martie replied.
David burst out in laughter. Thaddeus walked out shaking his head, accusing David and his mama of being too inappropriate for him.

Martie called Thaddeus a prude. "Just like his ole stuck-up mama," she whispered, before grieving, "Granny's gone baby."

David grabbed Martie's hand, "I know mama."

"I'm gonna miss her so much," Martie lamented. "We just talked last night. Thaddeus said I must have been dreaming, but it was so real. We talked about everything. We even got into an argument."

"What y'all argue about mama?"

Martie sighed deeply and wiped her red nose with the tissue. She sniffled and shook her head like she didn't want to say what they argued about. She squeezed David's hand, "Baby, I know you're grown, but you will always be my child. My baby. My titty baby," she said, digressing in her conversation. "Did you know you were five years old when you stopped breastfeeding?"

With a flat affect, David replied, "I wish I didn't know that, and mama, please don't tell anybody that."

"Well, granny told me to let you breastfeed until you stopped, and that's when you stopped. Whenever you couldn't sleep, titty helped you go to sleep. You would latch and the next thing I knew, you would be out like a light."

Aggravated, David got up to leave and Martie grabbed his arm, "I'm sorry baby. I just didn't want to do this…not now."

"Do what mama?"

Martie whispered, "Last night…Gertie Mae told me to tell Larry Jr. that you—"

"That I'm his son?" David excitedly interjected.

Martie pouted, "Why do you sound so happy about that?"

"Because it's about time mama."

"No…it's not," Martie whined.

"Why not woman?"

"Because…"

"Because is not an answer," David whispered.

"Because you're *my* baby."

David teasingly comforted Martie telling her that she was his baby too. "You know you'll always be my sweetheart and the love of my life…and the *pain* in my…heart."

Martie pushed David, "I know what you wanted to say…but you're the pain in the ass. You make me feel like I've been pregnant for twenty-one years straight…looking just like him too…"
Martie promised, for David's sake, that she would tell Larry Jr., but it would have to be after the funeral and most likely after her birthday. Her thirty-sixth birthday was supposed to be special, and she didn't want to ruin it by dealing with Larry Jr.

GOODBYE, QUEEN

Gertie Mae had no brothers, sisters, or even cousins that she claimed. She lived alone and was found alone, sitting in her recliner with the phone receiver in her hand. A desperate woman in need of Gertie Mae's help couldn't reach her by phone, so she went to her house without an appointment. She looked through the window curtain and saw Gertie Mae sitting in the recliner, but she wouldn't answer the knock. That's how the neighbors found out Gertie Mae had died. The morgue needed the signature of the next-of-kin to release the body, and the funeral director needed personal information on Gertie Mae. Just like everyone else around Ville

Platte, the funeral director only knew what others knew—Gertie Mae was the woman you went to whenever you had a problem. Her medicine was strong. Martie knew more about Gertie Mae Fontenot than anybody else. She was born, Viola Gertrude LeVeaux, on March 19, 1917, in Marksville, Louisiana. She was fourteen years old and pregnant when she arrived in Ville Platte. There, she met Sturdy Fontenot, a twenty-five-year-old man with his own home and land. He married her and was with her when she gave birth to a baby girl, whom she named Sylvia Ann. At fourteen, Sylvia Ann ran off with a thirty-year-old man named Larry Broussard. Gertie Mae gave birth to her second child, a son, whom she named Samuel, who *mysteriously* died when he was just ten years old. Everything in Gertie Mae's heart said Sturdy had something to do with Samuel dying so suddenly. She knew Sturdy was jealous of Samuel. He'd already accused her of loving Samuel more than she loved him. She threatened Sturdy with a promise, that if he had anything to do with her child's death, he wouldn't live another year. Sturdy died six months later and unfortunately, so did Sylvia Ann—she was only twenty-five years old. By age forty, Gertie Mae was a widow and childless. For years, she was bitter and became known by many in Ville Platte, as the bitter old witch. That's what she was called when Martie ran into her at the vegetable market that day. Martie was five years old. Larry Jr. was chasing her and she ran right into Gertie Mae, nearly knocking her carry basket out of her hand. When Larry Jr. recognized his grandmother, he rushed into her arms, and as soon as they finished hugging, Martie looked up at Gertie Mae and asked her if she could be her grandmother too. Gertie Mae chuckled and called Martie the most precious thing she'd ever seen.

Then she said, *"For sho baby doll…I'll be yu granmama."*

And so, she was until Martie was twelve years old. That's when Louise packed up the family and moved them to Beaumont, Texas. By then, Larry Sr. had already had his way with Martie, and had Larry Jr. not caught his daddy in the act, it would have continued. When Larry Jr. caught his daddy having his way with Martie, he beat that man within inches of his life. He beat him from the bedroom, through the kitchen, and into the backyard. All Larry Sr. could do was holler, and try to run, but he couldn't get away because his pants were around his ankles. After Larry Jr. finished beating his daddy, he went inside and got that .32 caliber pistol, but by the time he came back out, Louise had made it home. She covered that man's naked body at the risk of exposing her own sanctified nakedness. She begged Larry Jr. not to kill his daddy and the only reason he didn't is because Louise was in the way. Gertie Mae once told Martie that many people warned Louise about Larry Broussard before she married him, but she wouldn't listen. Some people believed that Larry Broussard did right by Sylvia Ann because she ran off with him. However, Gertie Mae knew the only reason Sylvia Ann ran off with Larry Broussard was because she didn't understand what he did to her was wrong. He caught that child one afternoon on her way home from the store, lured her just off the roadside into the woods, and tore into her innocence. Despite how she came into the world, Sylvia Ann was cursed with that thing that makes a man's lust untamable. She was a beautiful girl, and a shapely little woman. Larry Brousard was the same man he'd always been, but the day Louise saved his life, Gertie Mae promised Martie that he would never harm her, or any other young girl ever again. She said she would see to it. Shortly after Louise got everyone settled in Beaumont, word came that Larry Sr. had lost his mind. All he was doing in Ville Platte, was walking around day and night. He didn't change his clothes and he wasn't eating. He was in bad shape, and within a week from that report came another—Larry Sr. was found dead in a cow pasture. They said he was so small, that he weighed less than a child. The word around town was that the bitter old witch was the one who cursed him. It was true. Gertie Mae's medicine was strong. She knew so much and had taught Martie much of what she knew, but Martie's tender heart hindered much of what she learned. Before being taught by Gertie Mae, Martie had only heard stories of women putting their periods in red gravies and feeding it to their lovers. She'd never heard of the other things women could do with their spit, urine, breast milk, and vaginal fluids from self-pleasure. While many women swore by the power of their periods, Gertie Mae promised a woman's breast milk and vaginal fluids from self-pleasure is more powerful than her red waste. With what she called, clean fluids, a woman could create an unbreakable bond with her boychild, and if used correctly, could keep a son from becoming a man like his no-good-daddy. However, fragrances and teas were two of Gertie Mae's favorites. She taught Martie, that if a woman keeps her scent in a man's nose, she will always be on his mind. When it came to Black, Martie learned how to reverse that. To Black, Martie had a rather peculiar odor that he couldn't stand at times, but he loved that smell on their neighbor, Brenda Faye.

After burying a pair of Black's underwear in Brenda Faye's backyard, he eventually found his way into Brenda Faye's bed. It was too bad Brenda's husband didn't find out when it first happened because Black would have been killed much earlier—though he was dying slowly anyway. He'd been sick from the devil's breath Martie blew into his nostrils every time he was passed out drunk. Black was losing his mind because Martie had wrapped some of his hair in pork fat and placed it in an ant bed. The man couldn't think straight unless he was drunk, which is why he was drinking himself to death— passing blood every time he sat on the toilet.

But there the queen lay, in a bronze casket with gold rails. Everything was surreal—and final. She was only seventy years old, and the funeral home had done a wonderful job preserving the woman who was more like a mother to Martie. They managed to keep her lips tight, almost to a pucker, which is exactly the way she held her mouth most of the time—except when she laughed. She had such a gorgeous laugh, Martie recalled. It was deep, with a purring sound at the end. A laugh that would make you think she was something else in her younger days—a real hot mama. But that couldn't be farther from the truth. Though brown-skinned and beautiful, she'd been without a companion for thirty years and never had the relationship she so deserved.

A simple graveside service was all Gertie Mae would have wanted. She never enjoyed lots of attention, but Martie couldn't just send her away like that. There were just too many people who benefitted from her medicine. Men and women who desired to keep their lovers, people hoping to break hexes from their family members, and countless women who desired to collect early life insurance settlements from their no-good husbands. She deserved to be sent away nicely. As the priest prayed the final prayer before committing Gertie Mae's body to the earth, Martie's heart convinced her that Gertie Mae had never steered her wrong. There had never been a single moment when she distrusted Gertie Mae, and even though, what she wanted her to do was still hard, deciding to go through with it was a little easier. As the crowd disbursed, a woman approached Martie, and expressed her condolences. She asked Martie if she was Louise Landry's daughter. Martie confirmed Landry was Louise's maiden name, but that she was a Ulyss, and then a Broussard. The woman excitedly expressed that she thought Martie looked familiar, but that she remembered her from a little girl.

"I'm Edna. Clement was my brutha," she said.

"My daddy?" Martie squeaked. "I didn't know I had an aunt."

Surprised by Martie's words, Edna questioned, "Yu mama neva mention Clement brothas and sistas?"

"No ma'am," Martie answered.

"Whatchu say?" Edna questioned, before sharing that it was six of them altogether, "Fo guls and it was Clement and our brotha, Willie," she said. Edna claimed Louise grew up close with the family, and that they all knew each other long before she and Clement were married. As teenagers, they all worked in Mr. Frank Duplechan's Garden. She chuckled at the memory of how all the men who came to Mr. Duplechan's market were crazy about Louise because she was so pretty.

"Speshly dat Mista Duplechan," she said. "Dat man wud give Louise jus about anythang she ask him fo. Do yu rememba Mr. Duplechan, wit dem light green eyes?"

"No ma'am. I don't remember him, but I do remember the fruit and vegetable market," Martie confirmed. "It's actually where I first met Granny Gertie."

"Yaa, well, thas the same family. All his daughters thank they run everything. But anyway, that wuz way befo my brotha married Louise."

Thaddeus interrupted, and reminded Martie that they needed to get back to Beaumont. He pointed, to show her that David and Larry Jr. were already pulling out. Martie quickly brought the conversation to an end, and assured Edna that she wanted to meet her daddy's family. She promised to tell her mom, they met.

"Be sho tuh tell yu mama we met, ok?" Edna requested.

Before heading to Beaumont, David and Larry Jr. stopped for gas, a Big Red soda, and a cup of ice for Larry Jr's cognac. While inside the store, David saw a white woman who looked so much like his mom, he did a double take. She had the same eye and hair color. The only differences were her skinny nose and a slightly flatter backside. Otherwise, they were the same height, build. David hesitated to approach her, but when she saw him and gave a friendly smile, he felt comfortable enough to approach her. He asked if he could show her a picture, and when she said it was ok, he showed her the picture of himself and his mom. He handed the woman the picture and watched her reaction.

Her eyes widened, "I can see this is you, but who is the woman?" she asked.

"That's my mom," David answered. "At first glance, I thought you were my mama."

"Is she…still alive?"

"Yes, ma'am. She is," David answered.

"Oh, my" the lady responded. "Do you guys live here?"

"No ma'am. We live in Beaumont, but my mom lived here when she was a little girl."

"How old is your mom?" she asked.

"Thirty-six," David replied.

"Oh, wow, she's three years older than me," The lady answered, her face reddening. "Let me see that picture again. What's your mom's name?"

"Martha Malcolm. Well, it was Ulyss when she lived here. My grandmother was married to a Ulyss," David explained.

"Oh, okay. Well, my name is Lisa Duplechan. It was nice meeting you."

David introduced himself and watched Lisa as she went to her truck. Larry Jr. did a double take when he saw her, because she really favored Martie. Meanwhile, Thaddeus and Martie were on their way back to Beaumont. Thaddeus did most of the talking while Martie did most of the thinking. She obsessed over the reason Louise never mentioned her dad's family, and why after thirty-six years she met an aunt for the first time. In the background of her thoughts, she heard Thaddeus rambling about some of the people at the funeral, and how they gave him the *willies.* He was saying something about being there was like being in a place that didn't feel right, and how he just had a weird feeling. He shifted and spent a few moments talking about how much David looked like his uncle, how they even walked alike, and how he didn't notice it until he saw them together.

"Did you notice that?" He asked.
Martie ignored the question on purpose, acting like she was in deep thought—much deeper than she was.

"Hey," Thaddeus called.

"Huh?" Martie answered, as she looked at him.

"Did you hear anything I said?"

"No, baby. I'm sorry. I guess I just zoned out," she claimed. "What did you say?"

"Nothing important," Thaddeus replied, before drifting into silent mode.
Martie expected to see David when they made it home, but he wasn't there. She was fine with him not being home, but that was before Thaddeus was called in to cover someone's shift. She paged David. When he called back, he said he was still with Larry Jr. but refused to say where they were. Martie whined about not wanting to be alone for the night, and asked if he could come and stay the night. David's silence proved she was interrupting his

plans, but she didn't care. He sighed before covering the phone with his hand to say something. Martie strained to make out what he was saying, but she couldn't. A few seconds later, he said he would be right over.

"And tell your daddy to drop you off," Martie requested, but David had already hung up.

When he arrived, it was some woman dropping him off. With a little attitude, Martie asked why Larry Jr. didn't drop him off.

With a little attitude, David answered, "For what? I thought you wanted me to come over here. I'm here." He kissed her forehead, but it was more like a push with his lips. "If you want to creep with my daddy just keep me out of it," he said.

"Boy…don't nobody want your triflin ass daddy. I wanted to talk to him about you."

David's pitch went higher, "Well, how come you ain't just say that? I could have just told him you needed to talk to him. Do you want me to call him now? He's right there at the Holidome."

"No!" Martie snapped.

"Are you sure?" David questioned.

"Yes, I'm sure. I don't want him coming over here by himself. It would have been better if y'all came together. That's what I was telling you that but you hung us so fast." Martie scowled, "And what were y'all doing at the Holidome anyway?"

"Nuthin," David replied, smiling.
His smile turned her stomach, and David knew it did.

He teased her, "I look just like him huh?"

"No," Martie replied. "I think you're much more handsome."
David could tell his mom was having difficulty resolving her emotional conflict, but he could also see that she liked being able to say, *'Your daddy'* when she talked to him. It felt pretty good to him too. Martie sighed, as her eyes suddenly glossed over.

David drew closer, "What's wrong mama?" Martie asked David again, how he truly felt about her planning to tell Larry Jr. the truth. He answered as he did before. He was cool with all of it. She asked if he'd already talked with Larry Jr. about the situation and he promised he hadn't.

"David, don't lie to me," Martie begged.

"C'mon mama…You know I wouldn't do that to you," David assured.

"I know you wouldn't. Do you think he already knows or suspects?" She questioned.

"I don't think so," David answered. "He may…feel…think…but, I don't know."

"Why you say that?" Martie wondered.

David explained, "The way he looks at me sometimes. Like today, driving back…we were talking about boxing. And…it was just the way he was looking at me. It was like a proud daddy look…like Mr. Sammy used to look at me."

Martie groaned, sickened. She whined, "I just don't want to lose my baby."

"Never," David promised. "But I am ready for us to know each other as father and son, and I'm sure he'll be excited too. And then we can—"

"Whoa, whoa, whoa. Slow down, mister," Martie warned.

"What mama?"

"Baby, it's not gonna be like that. It can't be like you're thinking," Martie corrected.

"What do you mean?" David questioned.

"Baby, when I tell Larry Jr. this, it's not like you two can just be open with this," Martie warned.

David questioned, "Why not?"

Martie explained, "For one, your grandmother. Can you imagine what would happen? Shoot, Thaddeus said something today that caught me off guard. On our way back to Beaumont, he said that he never noticed how much you look like Larry Jr. until he saw y'all together. He said you two even walk alike."

"And what did you say?"

"Nothing. I acted like I didn't hear him. That's why I say this still can't be an open thing," Martie clarified.

"That's fine mama. But like I was about to say. I'm sure he'll be excited to know I'm his son and not his nephew. Then we can deal with how I got here. Mama, I still don't like how I got here. I mean, I'm glad to be here…but I still don't like what he did to you. So…once you tell him…I want to hear him apologize…to you and me. And, if he don't…then you know…hey…psst…that nigga can go on about his business. It's still me and you. Right?"
Martie felt David's words deep in the pit of her stomach. What he said was clear, but Martie knew how bad her son wanted a life with his daddy.

GAMES

Tina's head was already full of junk because she hadn't heard from David since he left campus, and the junk Sydney brought back from Easter weekend only made it worse. Sydney spilled David's drama like it was the thing to do—talking about how much David had changed. She expressed how disappointed she was in him because of the things he'd been involved in, and for the type of females he'd been with. She even told Tina she needed to wake up to who she was dealing with. Tina believed some of the things Sydney shared, but she already knew David had been with other girls. He was a hot guy. Why wouldn't he, she reasoned. Furthermore, it wasn't like they were together, together. On the other hand, Tina felt some of the things Sydney mentioned sounded more like deliberate sabotage, and if there was one thing Tina learned from her dad, it was that she should always consider the source. In Sydney's case, she was a jealous female who craved attention—which she never lacked. Her name was probably on every guy's hit list on campus. Therefore, it frustrated her to know David was attracted to someone she considered to be beneath her. When David finally called Tina, his version of everything Sydney had told her was much different. His version was more believable, and just like Tina shared with him about Sydney, David confirmed she was the same way in school—always pouring salt on a female she didn't like.

Tina had to ask, "Did you two spend some time together?"

"Yeah," David answered. "She came to my apartment. She was there when I found out my great-granny died."

"Yeah, she did mention that. I'm sorry for your loss," Tina consoled.

"It's cool," David claimed, adding that he was in Louisiana for the entire week.
Tina probed, asking if it was necessary to ask if anything happened between him and Sydney. Condescendingly, David told her no, she didn't need to ask, but Tina asked anyway and David's brief silence was the answer she didn't want to hear. However, David knew Sydney well enough to know she wouldn't admit to being intimate, especially not with her having a boyfriend. So, David denying anything happened was a safe response.

Tina asked, "Would you tell me if it did?"

"Well, I can tell you this, if we were together, I wouldn't have to…because I wouldn't cheat," David promised.
Tina was speechless, and though she had other questions about that Easter weekend, David's answer made all of them seem irrelevant. She changed the subject and asked about his plans for the coming weekend. She invited him to their track meet at UT, in Austin, knowing Sydney didn't invite him, because Kenny was going with her. Tina had overheard Sydney mentioning that Kenny was going to be meeting her parents.

"It sure would be nice to see you," she said.

David asked, "What about your parents?"

"They may not come…but if they do, I guess you can act like you went to support your friend," she plotted.

When the weekend arrived, David kept his Friday night routine with Ara but broke his Saturday morning routine at Rosalind's. He told her he was heading to Austin and would return home around six-thirty or seven that evening. He arrived at UT early, but it was already a disaster when he arrived. Seeing Kenny sitting with Sydney's parents caught David off guard. He realized in that very moment, that was probably the reason Sydney didn't even mention their track meet, and perhaps why Tina invited him. He chuckled at the thought, and put on his game face, still thinking that because of he and Sydney's Easter weekend, Kenny meeting her parents was put on permanent hold. However, the family group was just as surprised to see David too. Neither Sydney's parents nor Kenny knew David would be there. Acting as normal as possible, David greeted Mr. Sidney with some dap and kissed Mrs. DeDe on the cheek, but closer to the corner of her lips, like they always kiss. Mrs. DeDe introduced David as if she was concerned about Kenny's feelings. She said David was like her son and that he and Sydney had grown up together like brother and sister. She was surprised when Kenny mentioned they'd already met when David visited the campus.

Kenny greeted, "What's up man?"

David replied, "You bruh. You aight?"

"Fo sho," Kenny replied.

David sat to Mr. Sidney's left and Kenny remained at Mrs. DeDe's right. Tina's parents were in the stands, not far away. They were two rows up and farther to the right of where they were sitting. The Hicks' saw David when he entered the stands, but David didn't see them until he got settled and looked around. Mrs. Hicks was already looking at him when his eyes met hers. He waved, unsure if she or her husband would speak back. They didn't. He shrugged it off, knowing Tina would catch some flak for him being there. After Tina's events, she did get some tension from her parents. Despite telling them David was there for his friend, Sydney, Tina's parents called the situation an unfortunate coincidence. The fact Tina was at a college farther away from home, and knowing David had connections at the same college, didn't sit well with them. They preferred Tina and David to reside on different planets if it were an option. Tina's hopes of *seeing* David that day only happened through a few accumulated glances in his direction. Getting any congratulatory hugs and smooches was definitely out of the question too.

Sydney on the other hand deserved an Oscar for how well she balanced her scenario—talking with her parents, her boyfriend, and the *best friend* she'd just recently spent the night with. David bit down on his jaws the whole time they interacted, letting Sydney know he thought she was foul. Sydney bucked her big eyes at David, letting him know he wasn't any better. While they all talked, Kenny fired the first shot. He asked David why he wasn't over there talking to his girl, Tina, and Sydney burst out laughing, knowing exactly why. Her outburst stung, but he explained to DeDe, whom Kenny was talking about, by mentioning the incident that happened in Baytown.

"Oh, thas the gul you was wit when that happen?" DeDe whispered.

"Yes, Ma'am," David replied.
After that matter was settled, David decided to be messy too. He asked Kenny if he and Sydney set a date for their wedding.

DeDe balked, "Hmph. I don't thank so! Sydney betta sit huh-self down somewhaa…and finish school befo she even thank about marryin somebody."

Sydney snapped, "Mama, ain't nobody said nothing about no marriage. David is just being messy."

"Well, he betta be," DeDe promised.

Sydney rolled her eyes, "You make me sick," she snarled.

David laughed, knowing exactly what she meant by her, *'you make me sick'* statement. He asked if she needed a doctor, and she responded by giving him the pointer finger, which was her way of giving him the middle finger.

David teased, "Back atcha."

Mr. Sidney mumbled, "There they go…having another lover's quarrel."

"Daddy, stop it!" Sydney balked, "And David, you go home." When David got up to leave, Sydney's heart dropped. She didn't mean for him to leave, and David knew she didn't, but he said his goodbyes anyway, forcing her to sit there and act as if she wasn't bothered. On his way out of the stadium, David wished he could get close enough to whisper a hello to Tina, but he couldn't.

He sent a message through Connie, "Tell my girl feel her."

It was five-thirty when David made it home. He had twelve missed calls, but only five messages. One message was from Piggy, asking if she could come and spend the night. Martie left two messages, checking to see if he'd made it back from Austin. She wanted him to return her call. Strangely,

Rosalind had left two messages, breaking her own rule. She disguised her voice on the first message, but the second one, she was extremely bold. She said she was upset because it was the third Saturday that he'd stood her up. She understood the reason for the other two Saturdays, but putting her on the back burner for a track meet was not good. She said she would be at his apartment at seven that evening, but she arrived at six on the nose. She came inside with an ultimatum—either he was going back to Galveston with her, or she was about to get what she came for right then. Rosalind had always carried herself like a lady—instructive, intuitive, and keenly aware of her power, but she was tipsy, greedy, and unusually aggressive. She was out of character, acting like a dark-skinned Ara, minus the pre-game expletives. Aggressively, she mounted, took the reins, and took control of her destiny, but in another position, she was quickly humbled by merciless gut punches. She attempted to reduce the forceful impact; first with her hand, and then by twisting her hips to one side. Still, it felt like Daid was rearranging her insides. Rosalind released a savage growl as David's pace increased, putting her in full cat-back pose. She anticipated him reaching his limit with her, shrieking, holding on for as long as she could, but lost it before he climaxed. Her body convulsed, but when David finally reached what he worked so violently to accomplish, it deceived him. It was mechanical. It just happened, with no feeling. It just shot. Rosalind slowly lowered herself onto her stomach and then the fetal position. Her insides were traumatized and confused—glad it was over. For the first time in their history Rosalind didn't praise David's performance. She just got up and silently dressed without taking a shower. David put on a pair of shorts and sat quietly on the edge of the bed with his elbows on his knees, looking down at the floor. Rosalind's feet appeared in his line of sight, and she firmly cupped David's jaws and lifted his face.

She looked him in the eyes and expressively warned, "Don't you ever…and I mean ever…do that to me again. Do you understand?" The seriousness in Rosalind's voice made David want to say, yes ma'am, but he grabbed her wrist and kissed the palm of her hand. He apologized but confessed he'd only done what he thought she wanted him to do, because of how aggressive she was. Rosalind let out a deep sigh, knowing the apology was sincere. She owned up to her perceived aggressiveness, and confessed it definitely wasn't her thing. She planted a soft truce on his lips and was about to leave on the agreed terms when the phone rang. Rosalind stopped and looked at David while it was ringing, wondering if he was going to answer or let the answering machine pick up.

She quickly interjected, "If that's another woman, I don't want to hear her voice. Answer the phone please."

David quickly grabbed the receiver before the answering machine picked up. He just held the phone for a moment, until Rosalind urged him with her eyes to go ahead and talk.

He answered, "Hello…hey sis…girl, I just got back…yes, I did…yes, I was gonna call you back…as soon as I finished…none of your business…No…no, just tell him I'll come get you…yes, girl, I promise…girl, I'll be there…bye…bye Piggy…ok…I'll see you in a few…bye."

David hung up the phone and Rosalind slowly turned and walked out. Midway down the stairs, she said she would call to let him know she made it home safely.

"Hey. Hey." David called.

Rosalind didn't look back right away, but waited until she reached the driver's side of her car, "What, Mr. Malcolm?"

David kissed his two fingers and blew her a kiss goodnight.

Rosalind shook her head, smiling, "You are such a mess. Goodnight."
The following weekend, Sydney managed to get away from Kenny, bringing Lydia with her to make things look legit. She claimed she was going to support Lydia for something that was going on with Lydia's family, but they came and camped out at David's apartment—interrupting his entire weekend. They held him hostage, ate his food, took over his bed and turned his apartment into a dorm room. He loved every bit of it—especially seeing his best friend and her best friend, walking around in all their fineness. Facially, the two looked nothing alike, but they were built similar. From behind, they were double-mint twins. The only thing David didn't enjoy about that weekend, was finding out why Tina hadn't taken his calls since the track meet in Austin. Sydney said it was because of Tina's parents. They threatened she not have a single occurrence of her talking with David, or him being on campus around her. They had gone so far as to inform Coach Johnson, the dorm matron, and campus security that there should be no communication between her and David. Campus security actually had a photo of him. It sounded like a restraining order, but Sydney thought it was funny. She told David not to worry, because he could do so much better than Tina, and

didn't have to lower his standards so much. Yet, she was still dating Kenny, while planning to spend her upcoming birthday with David. After the long weekend, Sydney and Lydia left happy that they'd pulled off a successful caper, but her schedule soon conflicted with David's, hindering other plans to spend time with each other. Once again, their communication dropped off, making it easier for David to settle into his regular, weekly routine. However, when he qualified to compete in the 1987 Pan American Games in Indianapolis, Sammy put him on lockdown—no calls, no visits, and no sex. Martie accompanied David to Indianapolis and spent the entire fifteen days with him. She was his motivation—all he needed to dominate his weight class. The Cubans put up some stiff competition, but the U.S. team came out victorious and David took home his second gold medal.

"Eighty-eight Olympics!" David blasted, believing he was a prime candidate for the Olympic team, but it was apparent someone else thought differently.

David's national titles and gold medals weren't impressive enough for sponsorship. He wondered if it was because he didn't belong to the right boxing club. Self-financing was an option, but the red tape associated with it would be the biggest challenge.

David was willing to meet the challenge. He was
hungry. He was desperate. He argued for it, but
Sammy argued against it. It was possible for him to
get endorsements if he competed. His life as he
knew it could change overnight. Everything he
wanted to do for his mom would happen, Sammy
confirmed. No one had confidence in David's ability
more than Sammy, but he honestly shared that it was
a strong possibility that things wouldn't work out as
planned. There were no refunds.

Sammy looked into David's eyes and promised,
"Once you invest that money, it's gone. Then what?
Wait and try again in 1992? By then you'll be twenty-
five years old, and top rank boxing has a short life
span son…trust me," Sammy pleaded.

"So, what should I do?" David wondered.

"We can turn pro and cover some ground and
build up your record, and when those Olympic
champions turn pro, he'll have to come through
you."

David reluctantly agreed to do it Sammy's way, and
Sammy established Championship Management
Group and signed a management contract with
David. He made David the sole stockholder of
David Malcolm, Inc., and convinced him to invest
everything he had into CMG. In a matter of a few
weeks, David was licensed and through some

connections in the business, was contracted to fight Manuel Zavalla, who was ranked third in the WBA. Zavalla was considered the most vicious in their weight class—a true brawler. The payout was forty thousand, which Sammy claimed was above top pay for David's rank. To sweeten the deal, the winner of his fight was guaranteed a consideration of negotiation to fight Klaus Heimoway for the title. Zavalla was the favorite, but when David stopped Zavalla in a fifth-round TKO, he didn't get that consideration of negotiation for the title as mentioned. The powers that be wouldn't let that happen so quickly. The honor went to the number two ranked, Erol Bryson, who surprised everyone when he knocked Heimoway through the ropes in the third round—clenching the title. Sammy returned David's investment money, but the forty-thousand CMG collected covered all of David's expenses—his taxes first, and then his management and training fees. Fifty percent of the balance was placed in a company expense account, and Sammy gave David a brand new ten-thousand-dollar stack. David flipped out about his money. Sammy tried his best to explain to David how that he was the business and that the business was him, to no avail. He further explained that David Malcolm, Inc. is managed by CMG and that CMG takes care of him.

"But that's my money to do what I wanna do with it," David argued.

"Right," Sammy agreed. "It's all your money. The money in the expense account is your money. The ten thousand dollars in your hand is your money. Trust me."

"I do, but that's my money, Mr. Sammy! What if I want to buy my mama a house?"

"Then CMG will write a check for what you need son. It's still your money. All of it is your money. All I'm doing is assuring you have something when you fight your last fight." Sammy promised.

David wasn't getting it, so Sammy sat him down and told his story, blow for blow—sharing how his career ended. Hands down, Sammy owned the heavyweight ring in the sixties. He wrecked everyone who'd gotten into the ring with him, but when certain powers wanted a new champion, Sammy was offered money to throw a fight. He didn't want to throw the fight, so his career was threatened if he didn't. He was given the option to retire, but he wasn't in the best financial condition—he'd wasted a lot of money.

"Long story short, I took every single penny to my name and placed a backdoor bet on myself and I beat *the hell* out of Jerry Cone. I made some money that night, but when it was all over, I lost everything that mattered—my son, my belt, four years of my life, and most of all, my good name. Those bastards planted drugs on my bus and falsified my medical records to say I had drugs in my system, and they robbed me of everything—except for the little money I had. So, this is why I'm trying to show you how to take care of your money now. I want you to be able to walk away from the ring *whenever* you're faced with something like that…and I promise you, son, at some point, someone will approach you with an option. I want you to be able to walk away." David sat quietly hanging on every word that fell from Sammy's lips. What he said was scary, and it made sense—sort of. To test Sammy's claim, David requested all of the money from his expense account so he could give it to his mama, to hold for him.

When Sammy reluctantly agreed to give it to him, David replied, "Good. Because I wanna buy my mama something really nice. And I want some wheels."

David took his mom shopping and bought her a new wardrobe, and a brand-new living room and dining room set. He bought the car he fell in love with at first sight—a black-on-black 1985 Cutlass 442 with T-tops and chrome Crager rims. He named it Ghost.

OLYMPIAN

Sydney and Lydia received their invitations to the 1988 Olympic Trials. Sydney received hers for the 100 and 200 meters, and Lydia, the 400 meters. Sydney's life-long dream was coming true and things couldn't be more perfect for Lydia. They both owned their events and sealed their opportunity to represent the US Team in Seoul, Korea. Lydia captured the gold in the 400 meters and a silver in the 4x400 relay. Sydney made Beaumont, Texas proud when she brought home three gold medals—100, 200, and the 4x100 relay. Everything about that girl on television was beautiful—her stride, strength, and shooting the clock with her finger when she broke the record in the two hundred. The girl was ripped, but all woman in every way she moved. Her personality shined during her brief interviews—even more after being referred to as one of the sexiest Olympic athletes. Sydney Hebert become a household name—a brand. She was unexpectedly recruited by the prestigious, World Council of Professional Athletes before the Olympic closing ceremony. When she returned to Beaumont she was presented with a key to the city, and in another special ceremony on October 3, 1988, she signed her contract with the WCPA. She was assigned to the

Region 3 Management Group in Atlanta, Georgia, and a fancy, upscale suite at the Sheraton Suites became her temporary home—until her townhome in Alpharetta, Georgia was ready. While living at the Sheraton, Sydney signed a major shoe endorsement with Streak Running Shoes and a very lucrative sports drink endorsement with Swift. Julia Swinsenhauer, Sydney's agent and manager, secured several lucrative opportunities, including six commercials, compensation guarantees for competition, paid photo shoots, and speaking engagements at schools and universities. During a speaking engagement at the Paramount Elementary School, in Azusa, California, and fan, Vivian Wright, snagged a front-page photo with her favorite athlete. Her quote, "I want to be just like Ms. Hebert when I grow up" was published underneath the image. Sports magazine covers weren't the only place Sydney's face was plastered. As with other Olympians before her, the girl made it to the cereal box too, but David's favorite photo of her was the frontal view of her 200-meter gold. Sydney's eyes were locked on the tape but it looked like she was looking right into the camera. Silver medalist, Gabriella Lawson to her left, looked as if she was breathing on Sydney's shoulder, but she wasn't even close. Everyone watching that race from other angles could see at least a five-person gap between the tip of Sydney's trail foot and Gabriella. Life for Sydney and her parents as they'd always known it, changed drastically. The Pear Orchard section of Beaumont attracted too much attention for Sydney's parents, so she bought them a beautiful four-bedroom home on Nantucket Drive in the west end of the city. She offered them the chance to move to Georgia, but they agreed it would be best to visit, rather than pack up and leave. Sydney bought her dad a brand-new Ford F250 truck and a bass boat and trailer to go with it. She bought her mom that brand-new Cadillac she wanted and gave her money for a whole new wardrobe, but DeDe loved her tight polyester pants—they looked good on her hips. Sydney's running shoe commercials were some of the hottest sports commercials on television. The first one was in black and white. The setting was dark with the sound of breathing and multiple heartbeats. In the distance, the viewer could see dark figures, adjusting into their starting blocks. The sound of breathing gets louder and the heart beats become more rapid, and suddenly, there's a deep inhale right when a man's voice yells, "*SET!*" The runners raise their hips in slow motion and everything is silent. The gunshot, POW! Everything starts in super slow motion and the camera shows the Streak shoe symbol and then fades to black. It shows Sydney's calf muscle and fades to black. It shows her thigh muscle and fades to black. It shows her stomach muscles and fades to black. It shows her arms and shoulders and the side view of her face and fades to black, and suddenly the race goes full speed with sound effects—WHOOSH! Sydney's speed is ridiculous. The crowd is roaring as the camera pans out. They look like blurred silhouettes as Sydney blasts past them. The cameras flash like crazy as she crosses the finish line with the other runners trailing. Then there's a still shot of Sydney's nude side-view—from her hip down to the running shoe symbol. It fades to black again, and then the question appears: Do you have what it takes to streak? Another sound effect kicks in again as Sydney passes the camera—WOOMF! The commercial made you want to own a pair of Streaks—if for no other reason than to say, you own a pair. Sydney's second commercial was filmed in Los Angeles where she met Rondel Reese, the very distinguished, confident and handsome fifty-five-year-old regional manager. Although older than her dad, Rondel easily caught Sydney's attention at first sight, and interacting with him only made her realize her legitimate attraction to older men. It was similar to what she felt when she first met Lilo. Lilo had a serious calming effect on her. She felt safe underneath him and playfully assumed Rondel could easily make her feel the same way—if not better, but he was so professional. For the first two days of being on set, Sydney had only received a wink and a smile from Rondel. However, the day the commercial was finished, Sydney received an unexpected invitation from him to join him in his suite for champagne. Surprised by the unexpected invite, Sydney hesitated, thinking about the agency's fraternization policy. When Rondel explained that it only applied to managers and their direct clients, Sydney accepted but realized she'd done so without confirming whether Rondel was married or single. Thank goodness he volunteered his status as single and dating because Sydney wasn't sure if she would have been able to avoid the inevitable that was about to happen that night. Her flight back to Georgia was scheduled for noon the following day, so having a late-night tussle was no biggie she figured. In a sexy baritone, Rondel said he was looking forward to their evening. His voice sent chills dancing around Sydney's hips. Her stomach may have done a backflip too, but she didn't care. She was ready to embrace that evening head-on. It was her first-time sipping champagne in a hotel suite, with a man she'd only met three days prior. She recalled sipping from

Lilo's drink while they were in his hotel room, but that was because she needed to calm her nerves. She was cheating on Kenny with him. Being alone with Rondel was different. She was there because she was free to be there. She was relaxed. They toasted. The champagne warmed Sydney's skin and Rondel's sophistication and style made everything else hot. Everything had been hot since his invitation and Sydney knew exactly why she was there, but taking it slow—relaxing and talking was good. The conversation was smooth, though it was mostly about her. It was a little embarrassing being the main subject, but it was also intriguing because Rondel noticed *little* things about her; things only a best friend would pick up on. One of the things Rondel pointed out was how Sydney sometimes looked at a person's mouth while they were speaking instead of their eyes. He liked that. Sydney laughed and explained that she had a friend who did that to her. She thought it was weird of him, but also cute. She never knew why he did it though.

"Perhaps he wanted to kiss you," Rondel suggested.

He was right Sydney remembered. David was a kisser. He was more of a kisser than she was, and though she looked dreamily into Rondel's eyes, she didn't want to kiss him, but she couldn't stop his lips from touching hers. His lips were soft, but Sydney's mind pleaded, *no tongue, no tongue, no tongue,* and was delighted when Rondel pulled back without trying to give her tongue. Once again, she relaxed and inhaled Rondel's lingering fragrance. Fahrenheit was so befitting of the moment. Sydney felt herself overheating. She wanted Rondel to have her. She didn't want him to wait. She wanted him to do what he had invited her to his suite to do, and his response to her silent wish was right on time. He strolled to the king-sized bed and drew back the covers. He dimmed the lights and suggested the two of them get comfortable. Sydney nervously smiled at his confidence, figuring it was an older man thing. It drew her to him. She gazed into his eyes as he removed his shirt, exposing his well-defined, and hairy chest. Sydney swallowed, attracted, immediately wanting to bury her face against his chest and inhale, just as she did with Lilo. Instead, she lightly scratched his chest with her nails. Rondel reached behind Sydney's neck and loosened the string of her top. It folded down; exposing her beautiful youthfulness. They were small but confident—erect. Sydney's top fit tightly around her midsection, so she removed it, sparing the moment of any awkwardness. She undressed to her panties and slid between the cool sheets, lying on her side with her head propped on her hand, as if she were watching a show—smiling.

Rondel lifted Sydney's jeans from the floor and laid them neatly across the chair. *'Stike one,'* Sydney thought—embarrassed. He unfastened his belt and unbuttoned his pants before sitting on the bed to remove them. Sydney feasted on Rondel's broad shoulders. She reached and stroked her nails against his back. Rondel removed his pants and shorts and stood up, confidently exposing the back view of his fitness. He neatly laid his pants on the arm of the chair. Sydney smiled and threw back the covers as if she was saying—*surprise,* but when Rondel turned to face her, everything came to a screeching halt. It was like hearing a record scratch. Sydney's heart skipped a beat. She'd been enjoying the effects of the champagne bubbles, but those bubbles weren't making her see double.

Rondel was packing every bit of what she saw, and she sat straight up in the bed, "Oh no baby. We can't do this," she said.
Rondel had the biggest one she'd ever seen, and she quickly skirted out of the bed opposite Rondel.
"Ahn Ahn baby…this is not gonna happen," she promised. Rondel attempted to convince her that he would take his time, and be gentle, but there was no sweet-talking Sydney into trying to fight with that

monster. "Gentle is not the problem Rondel. That thing is not going to fit…anywhere," Sydney claimed. Rondel attempted to slow Sydney down, but she quickly cut him off, "I'm serious Rondel. This is not gonna happen," she promised, fearfully.

"Why darling?" he questioned.

"Uh…because I wanna have babies one day," Sydney claimed, knowing she didn't even like children.

Rondel didn't immediately give in. He tried to explain that he was not a rough man, but Sydney didn't care. She was nervous and scared. She wanted to leave, and she wanted Rondel to let her leave. It got worse when Rondel attempted to walk around to her side of the bed. It slapped against one thigh and then the other.

Sydney panicked, "Rondel! Do not bring that thing over here…I'm serious. I am not doing this, and I will scream!" she promised.

"Well, can you at least—"

"No!" Sydney snapped. "I don't want to touch it and I don't want it to touch me. I want to leave." Rondel finally backed off, assuring Sydney she was safe. He promised everything was fine. He didn't mean her any harm. He apologized with his palms facing Sydney, "I'll just…ease into the other section and you can get dressed," he said.

As Rondel cautiously moved inro the lounge section of the suite, Sydney didn't look directly at him, but from her peripheral, she confirmed her mind wasn't playing tricks on her. It was a beast. As soon as Rondel faded from view, Sydney hurried to the chair, grateful she still had on her panties. She grabbed her jeans and almost toppled as she hurriedly thrust her legs through. She danced into her top, skirting it over her jeans, and quickly tied the strings and left the room. She alternated between a jog and a skip to the elevator with her shoes in hand. By the time she reached the lobby, she'd regained some of her composure, but the driver, Andre, could tell something was a little off with her. He knew why he'd driven Sydney to Rondel's suite, and assumed Rondel had taken care of business, but he wasn't exactly sure. She'd only been up there for about thirty minutes, and Rondel's guests would normally be in his suite for a few hours. Sometimes overnight—recovering, Andre recalled. Everyone knew how Rondel handled business. Furthermore, Rondel was supposed to page him so that he would know when to bring the car to the rear exit. Andre was in a dilemma. He knew he couldn't just leave a client in an open lobby while he went to get the car, and it wasn't protocol to escort clients to the parking garage either. When Sydney insisted, they go, Andre nervously obliged. On the way to the car, Sydney started feeling a little lightheaded and figured it was the champagne but after she got into the car, the next thing she remembered was Andre telling her they'd arrived in her parking garage. Sydney sat for a brief moment, wondering how she missed a whole fifteen-minute ride. She felt weird. She could feel something wasn't right, but she couldn't tell what. She wondered if Rondel had put something in her drink. She recalled him popping the champagne bottle after she arrived at the room, and dismissed that thought, settling on perhaps that she'd just gotten too nervous. However, instinct provoked her to request to be brought to the hotel's front entrance. Sydney didn't care who saw her, but getting out of the car in that parking garage didn't feel safe. For all she really knew, she could have been in the same parking garage she had supposedly left from. Andre did as she requested and escorted her to her hotel room before leaving. The next day, Sydney flew back to Atlanta and Julia picked her up from the airport, sporting a big, cheesy-face grin.

"So…you met Rondel?" She asked, greedy for details.

"Yea…I met him," Sydney answered, still feeling weird about the encounter.

"And…how did it go?" Julia inquired, still smiling.

"How did what go?" Sydney asked.

"You know…" Julia egged.

"No, I don't," Sydney answered, avoiding Julia's probing.

"Ugh! All I wanna know is if it's really as big as some say. I heard it was huge," Julia mused.
Sydney lifted an eyebrow, knowing she couldn't tell Julia that it was as big around as her ankle, and midway his thigh, and that if she'd seen it in a picture, she would have thought it was fake.

Sydney gave Julia a safe and private answer, "I wouldn't know. I was there to shoot a commercial. Nothing more. Nothing less."

"Whatever. Anyway, I have a big surprise for you. Just wait til you see it. You are gonna love it!" Julia promised.

ENTANGLED

Julia drove past the exit for Sydney's hotel suite and continued north to Alpharetta, to a new development she referred to as the village—like the Olympic village, but much better. It was a section of beautiful townhomes owned by the WCPA.

"These are nice," Sydney admired.

"I'm glad you like it," Julia replied, as she pulled into a driveway and turned off the car.
Sydney followed Julia inside, thinking it was Julia's place, but when Sydney stepped in, Julia started a little presentation as if she were a real estate agent showing property.

"It's two stories. You have 3 bedrooms and 3.5 bathrooms. The main bedroom with a full bath is here," she pointed. "The half bath for the guests is there. The other two bedrooms and bathrooms are upstairs. You have a balcony with a wonderful view of the golf course and a comfy patio. You have a formal living area, a sitting room…we call it a lounge area, but you can call it an open office space, a reading room…you can put a day bed in there for company…whatever. I think it's a cozy space no matter what you do with it. Over here, you have a wonderful kitchen with a small island…and a nice open view. Your laundry room is there…and yes,

you have a washer and dryer. So, no trips to the laundromat. Yay…right? And through here and out this door is the two-car garage."
Julia opened the door and Sydney's shiny, red Volkswagen Jetta was parked inside— the one the WCPA gifted her when she signed her contract.

"Ta Da!" Julia sang. "Welcome to your new place, and guess what else? You have no rent."

"No rent?" Sydney repeated, surprised.

"No rent!" Julia confirmed, "The WCPA is *not* charging you anything to live here. It was all factored in through your endorsements. The only thing you pay is utilities and of course, the insurance…but anything that is not covered by insurance is also your responsibility, like damages from wild parties…yada, yada, yada, and that's for as long as you're here, or shall I say as long as you are actively contracted with the WCPA. There's no lease agreement on the townhome either. Well, there is a lease agreement, but it does not bind you to a time limit. You can move out anytime you choose and the furniture is yours also…you paid for it. Sounds like a great deal huh?"

"Uh…yea. You had me at no rent," Sydney replied.

"I know…right? The WCPA is freakin' awesome," Julia praised. "Well…if all is well and you like it…here's your keys to your new place and the keys to your new car. Oh, yeah, and one other thing, you have a personal assistant."

"A personal assistant?" Sydney repeated.

"Yea…trust me, you need one. Trying to keep up with everything that will be going on by yourself will drive you *crazy*. You'll get a chance to meet her at some point today. Her name is Pamela." Julia blew Sydney a kiss, "Bye now."

"Wait. Do I have to sign something?" Sydney wondered.

"You already did," Julia answered, as she walked out.

Sydney was alone. It was quiet. She looked left and right and up at the ceiling. She admired the furniture. She was impressed, though she wouldn't have chosen any of it—except for the plush, red sectional. "Now that, I love," she expressed, falling on it. She lay there looking at the ceiling, thinking how crazy things had been, and how fast things were moving. The doorbell chimed. Sydney crept to the front door and looked through the peephole at the brown-skinned woman with a ponytail, holding a box.

Sydney opened the door, "Pamela?"

"Yes ma'am. I'm your PA."

"Okay, Pamela…my PA. I'm not sure how all of this works, but…come in…"

Pamela stepped inside and asked where Sydney wanted the box that contained some mail, magazines, a few notepads, some ink pens, and a birthday card.

"I guess the coffee table would be fine," Sydney replied.

Pamela complimented the place as she walked confidently into the living area and sat the box down.

She smiled and admired Sydney. "I know you probably hear this at least a hundred times a day but I just have to say you are *so*…beautiful, and I love your hazel eyes."

"Thank you. But uh…including your compliment…that brings my total for the day up to about one," Sydney admitted.

"Nah…I can't believe that. Especially not after those hot commercials," Pamela complimented. Sydney smiled, but then her eyes glossed over, making the moment slightly awkward. She quickly apologized and asked Pamela to excuse her because things had been a little crazy. She hadn't been able to process the madness.

"It gets that way sometimes, but that's what I'm here to help with. I'm good at what I do," Pamela assured. "All you have to do is let me know what you need."

Sydney looked at Pamela with a blank stare, confirming she didn't know what she needed—especially not at the moment. She didn't know how any of it worked. She never had a personal assistant either. Pamela thought a second, and asked Sydney if she wanted to get out. Sydney thought for a moment and was about to decline the invitation until Pamela said she had an extra ticket to see Lilo Mims at the Warehouse in Atlanta.

Sydney experienced a classic Scooby-Doo moment, *Hurnh?* "Heck yeah, I wanna get out. What time are we leaving?"
The concert was at eight pm and Pamela's tickets were not just regular tickets. They were up close and personal tickets—like reach out and touch Lilo, close. The tickets were, see Lilo's face, clearly, close. They were Lilo making eye contact with you, close, and five minutes into the show, Lilo recognized Sydney and immediately acknowledged her, smiling ear-to-ear.

"Oh, my goodness, look at my beautiful friend. Come here. Come here," Lilo urged, telling stage security to give Sydney passage.
Sydney's heart was beating like it was about to beat out of her chest in excitement.

As soon as she gave Lilo her hand, he honored her, "Ladies and gentlemen…give it up for *my* friend…Sydney Hebert, America's 1988 Olympian."

The crowd applauded while Lilo looked at Sydney with such admiration. He flirted, "Isn't she just gorgeous?"
Sydney blushed and casually waved at the crowd as they applauded. Her tan jacket, white jeans, and tan-colored boots complimented Lilo's suit. The interaction almost looked staged but it was completely spontaneous. As the fans admired, Lilo excitedly revealed a secret—the mystery background vocals on his song, *I Miss You.*

"This is the beautiful face behind those vocals," he revealed, claiming, that the first time he heard her sing, he knew he had to get her to the studio. Sydney blushed almost to tears because no one knew she sang background vocals on that song, and she never told anyone. Kenny didn't even know Lilo had flown her back out to Georgia to do that. It was their secret, and now that secret was out. Lilo requested a mic for Sydney so that she could vibe with him for a moment. Lilo had done a remake of Marvin Gaye and Tammie Terrell's 1967 hit, *'If this world were mine,'* with a former Solara artist named Deja—who had been dropped from the label. The song was one of Sydney's favorites. She sang it often as if she was singing with Lilo. Unrehearsed and unplanned, Sydney sang with Lilo so naturally, it could have been their original. Their onstage chemistry amazed the crowd from beginning to end— ending with a kiss on the cheek and a bow. T-Bone, Atlanta's favorite radio jock boasted the following day how Sydney had done her thing on stage with Lilo Mims. He called her a songbird and newspapers echoed his words, and the very thing Lilo had mentioned the first time he met Sydney through Kenny, manifested. Rumors of Sydney's upcoming single sprang up immediately following the concert, and sales were already anticipated before an actual song was ever recorded. Sydney's interview in the February 1989 issue of *Jet Magazine,* alluded to a possible record deal, but she didn't confirm it. She didn't exactly deny it either, but the very next month when she returned from the indoor world championship in Budapest, Hungary, she signed a management contract with Lilo and a record deal with Solara Records. She recorded her first single, *Feel Me,* which was written and produced by Lilo. The song was released under the stage name, Tre´, short for Tre´vonne, Sydney's middle name., and was huge success. It received continuous rotation on the major radio stations in the south and mid-west. Majic 102 in Houston announced on the morning of

April 7th, that they would premier the new single by Tre´ at noon. David was washing Ghost when he heard it. It stopped him in his tracks. The song was beautiful from beginning to end. Sydney sounded like she was really in love. It made David's heart sick. Their widening timeline didn't make it any easier. Two months had passed since their last phone conversation. Six months had passed since the last time they saw one another in person, but when David received a page from a Houston number he didn't recognize, he started not to call it back but was glad he did. It was Sydney. She'd just checked into the Hilton in Houston because of an unexpected delay with her flight. One hour later David was in the lobby, waiting to be escorted to her room. It was almost comical seeing how Sydney's people were tripping over her. This was the same girl he grew up with and they were acting like she was a real celebrity, David thought. When he finally got to her room, he realized that's exactly what she'd become—a celebrity. She even had the little attitude to go with it— ordering folks around. She seemed to get off on everyone saying yes ma'am, no ma'am as they hopped to whatever she demanded, but as soon as her suite was clear of excess traffic, the girl he grew up with showed up. It was all smiles and hugs, and her goofily pushing him as she laughed. They immediately caught up on old news and shared some new news. The reason she hadn't been in touch was because life was crazy. Since they'd last seen each other in October, Sydney had been coast to coast—in and out of expensive hotels and restaurants. She'd met so many people—rich and famous. She'd even been asked out by some people they both knew from television. Kenny was completely out of the picture and had been for a while. She said things had gotten crazy with him. She didn't exactly share what happened but expressed how glad she was that it was over. David shared what had been going on with him, but the whole time he talked, Sydney sat there thinking about how badly she wanted to hump his brains out. She hinted at such with a devious look, but David tried to act like he didn't catch it. He kept talking—admitting the fruits of labor were coming in pretty slow for him. The only real payday was from his first fight, and ever since he turned pro, he fought regularly, sometimes to the brink of being excessive.

"But I have to. I gotta build up my record," he confirmed. David swore some of the boxers he fought were washed-up addicts, looking for a few extra dollars, but the side fights that Sammy set up were the toughest. Those had nothing to do with his boxing record though. They were straight money gigs. Some of them David knocked out in the first round, and others he had to fight, fight—seven and eight rounds of serious throwing down, he claimed.

"As far as payday for those fights, it's always a few grand for the winner…but the way CMG manages my winnings is another thing. From the get-go, they take out taxes, management, and training fees. Then they put fifty percent of that balance into an expense account and give me what's left. The expense account is my money too, but I have to ask for it when I need to do something," he admitted, searching for Sydney's thoughts about what he shared.

Sydney just sat there listening, but she was thinking about pouncing on him. She exercised some restraint and obliged his conversation by adding how similar his situation was to hers. She receives itemized reports each week, showing all expenses and who they're paid to. She bragged about the WCPA being top-notch but admitted the music side was very different. She was still trying to figure that part out, but she trusted Lilo and Solara was taking care of her.

"Shiiid mane…the WCPA seems like the way to go. Hook yo boy up?"

"Well…it doesn't exactly work like that. You don't approach them. They find you. It's like when scouts look at college athletes," Sydney explained.

"So, you're recruited?" David asked.

"Yeah, sort of…" Sydney answered, ambiguously.

"Well, since you're in there, you should be able to make a recommendation or something…right?" David wondered.

Sydney tightened her lips and stared at David without answering, hoping her silence would make him stop pushing. It didn't. He pressed again and she stopped him and told him how differently the WCPA operates from the average management company.

"Every professional athlete is not recruited by the WCPA. only certain ones, and from what I know, they do extremely thorough background checks; they interview college coaches and high school coaches, they consider education records, your amateur profile…whether or not you've been in trouble…if you're connected to someone who could be trouble…all that stuff. And if everything…is to their satisfaction, they'll contact you by letter. Someone may even call," Sydney explained.

"Sounds like the Country Club of the crème de la crème," David assumed.

"Right," Sydney answered, before telling David to shut up with the questions and to come indulge himself in some of her crème de la crème, or let her indulge in his. "Either way, come here," she requested.

David's smile faded, but he closed the few steps of distance between them and lay in her arms. She rubbed her nose against his before giving him a playful lip smack that turned into one of those kisses that felt like she was checking his tonsils. In a heated race, Sydney quickly liberated her shorts but David only managed to get his pants down below his knees before the two of them wrestled for dominance. David fought for Sydney's heart, but Sydney raced towards pleasure. In a blur, she got both of them to the finish line and laughed at what they must have looked like going at it the way they were. Afterward, Sydney encouraged David to stay focused on his boxing and not to worry about money. She assured him she was there for him and would look out for him if ever he needed anything. David pulled away, saying, he wasn't looking for a handout from her. Sydney insisted that's not what she meant. She promised she was only being the best friend she'd always tried to be. David assured her, as a best friend to him, he didn't think there could ever be a better one than her, but he shied away from telling her that he wished they could be more. He knew it was best to protect his heart because after she got on that plane, it would be a while before he would see her again. Sydney's new flight left a few hours later, and a few weeks after that evening, David received a credit card in the mail with a one-thousand-dollar limit. Sydney called him when she thought he'd received it and told him to use the card whenever he needed to use it and that she would pay the bill.

"No strings attached," she promised. Martie laughed when David told her what Sydney had done for him because she knew that was Sydney's way of keeping tabs on him.

Martie schooled him on not using that card for hotels, dinners for two, and especially not in women's department stores, "Unless it's something for me. I'm sure Sydney wouldn't mind you spending money on your mama," Martie assured. That was Martie's envy talking because every time she thought about DeDe's new life and where she lived, it made Martie feel like what she had was less than what she was worth. She'd finally gotten a new dining set, a new living room set, and a new air conditioner for that back room, but 2855 Houston Street still felt less than a home.

In regards to still having to drive the old faded Chrysler Cordoba, she was She was extra sick, "I could use another car too," Martie hinted. "Something sexy…like that white, sixty-six Mustang Earnest have down there. He's selling it you know?"

MY FIRST TIME

Feisty, foul-mouthed, and hot as a firecracker. Sydney was impressed with the half-pint diva she unexpectedly met during her trip to Cleveland, Ohio. Deja looked nothing like Lilo described when he called her a "short, nappy-headed, ugly lil something." Deja was cute and her hair wasn't nappy at all, but it was permed—short and tapered. She looked great in that tight, hot pink dress with a plunging neckline that ended at the top of her stomach. Her thick, caramel breasts looked like cantaloupes—all natural. Her lips, hips, and bumpers were straight attention-getters.

The way her lips wrapped around her words when she talked was enough to hold anyone's attention, and Sydney was attentive when Deja fired warning shots at Solara, "Be careful honey, because those are some tricks over there. All of them are no good. Domino may be the CEO, but that Lilo is a mother-f—er. He did a whoooole bunch of skeezers bad over there," she said, dragging out the word. She continued, "In case you haven't *heard*, that trick Lilo, had these *dumb*-ass females doing some desperate stuff for record deals, when the whole time it was for his own entertainment. Not one of those heffas got a real record deal." Deja rolled her eyes, "They thought they were gonna do me the same way, but I ain't the one," she said, pointing her finger with her white-tip nails. "My talent speaks for me and not what's between my legs...or behind my tonsils for that matter."

Sydney thought about Deja's words while she was on her knees about to give Lilo what he asked for. She had no earthly idea how to start, or even how to finish, but Lilo sat there like a king with his silk robe open, exposing his hairy chest and stomach. The way he sat there holding his glass of Cognac in one hand and twirling his fingers in Sydney's hair with the other was pure confidence. He expected to get what he wanted.

Sydney took Lilo in her hand and massaged, admitting, she wasn't sure how to do what he wanted, "I've never done this before," she confessed, seeking instructions.

Lilo's words dripped like honey when he told her to take her time and to just make love to it. She asked for a sip of his Cognac to calm her nerves and to boost her confidence. She swallowed, took a deep breath and exhaled. '*Ok. Just make love to it,*' she thought before going for it. Lilo laid his head back and groaned as soon as he felt Sydney's lips and when he did, she stopped and asked she'd done it too hard.

"No baby…that's good," Lilo whispered. Sydney started again, imitating the visuals she remembered from the porn videos she'd seen in college— except without the spitting and the choking. When she saw Lilo's hand, tightening around his glass, she was encouraged that she was doing it right. As she was comfortably progressing, doing it exactly as Lilo directed, an intrusive image of Uncle Denny's face flashed in Sydney's mind. She gagged and immediately heard a loud bang in her left ear. The next thing she knew, she was sprawled on the floor, lying on her side staring at the rain through the balcony glass. Lilo had slapped Sydney so hard that she was still trying to figure out what happened. Her face was stinging and Lilo was apologizing, saying he thought she was about to bite him, but Sydney just lay there on the zebra skin rug—in shock. With no additional comfort, or emotional assistance, Lilo just proceeded to have his way with her. He handled her while she was in shock; lying there silent, and motionless, until he finished. He fixed himself another drink and Sydney eventually got up and climbed into bed. The next morning, Lilo was out when she awaked. She took that opportunity to call David with the crazy idea of them spending both their birthdays together in Georgia, despite her busy schedule. Sarcastically, David asked what made her think that he would want to spend one week with her, let alone a whole month.

"Because you miss me, and because I miss my friend," she answered.

David playfully denied missing her, but Sydney begged anyway, "Please…with a lot of sugar on top…and a cherry too."

"Girl, you don't have a cherry," David teased.

Sydney smacked, "Boy, just come. Please…" David agreed he would come but only under one condition. He wanted a private concert.

"Done," Sydney agreed.

When Sydney told Lilo about her birthday plans, he claimed he didn't have a problem with David coming to visit, just as long as she understood David would not be staying at her place while he visited. Then he asked if David was the same guy who had come to her hotel room in Hoston. Sydney nervously answered, yes, but was shocked that he was bringing that up again. She'd already told him that her friend visited that day.

He continued, mentioning the cut-off blue jean shorts she wore while she alone with a dude in a hotel room, "Am I supposed to think y'all just hung out?" he questioned.

He called her sneaky and disrespectful, but Sydney quickly lied, "Nothing happened! I told you David is harmless," she claimed.

"I don't care!" Lilo snapped, admitting softly, that he didn't like the idea of any man being alone with his woman.

Internally, Sydney wondered exactly when she'd become his woman. She completely missed that conversation but she knew that was not the moment to debate that issue. She defended her friendship, admitting David was more like her brother, but Lilo didn't care about that either. She humbly protested that she would never put David in a hotel room for a whole month.

Lilo promised Sydney that David wouldn't be visiting for a month, "A weekend at most," he insisted.

Sydney attempted to remind Lilo that her and David's birthdays were nearly a month apart, but

Lilo stopped those words in her mouth when he firmly grabbed her cheeks.

He corrected her through clenched teeth, "I said…a weekend at most…and he will stay in a hotel. Now, how you two work out the particulars as far as who's paying for his taxi rides to and from, or who's paying for the car rental, or who's paying for his meals…I'm sure you two can work that out. Understand?"

A cold chill ran up and down Sydney's spine and she was almost afraid to blink, but she attempted to ask where all of his attitude was coming from, but he snapped,

"Hey! End of discussion dammit!"

Lilo stared at Sydney like he wanted to punch her in the face or something, and all of a sudden, for Sydney, Lilo's three-thousand-square-foot condo felt like it was reduced to the space she was standing in. She felt like she needed to ask permission to move, and didn't move until Lilo walked away first. Even then, she was so nervous that sweat from her underarms began rolling down her sides. She felt like a little girl who had just disappointed her dad, and wanted to apologize, but she didn't know what she had done to make him so angry. She quietly went to shower—a piping hot shower, to loosen her tense muscles. Lilo walked into the bathroom while she was air drying, and she grabbed the towel, wrapped and tucked. He came and stood behind her, causing her to lean her head forward as her muscles tensed up all over again. She felt like the boogeyman was behind her and was too afraid to turn around to see it. She folded her hands across her stomach while Lilo stood close behind her. She felt his breath on her neck, causing her to continue to hunch her shoulders—preparing to flinch. In a raspy voice, he asked Sydney if she loved the life she was living and the fame he had given her. Sydney didn't know how to answer that because one part had nothing to do with him. So, she didn't answer, until Lilo creepily asked if she was willing to pay the price to keep it.

"You know you owe me, right?" Lilo whispered, before snatching the towel off of Sydney—leaving her naked and trembling.
He hastily unbuckled his belt and Sydney nervously looked at him to see what he was doing, but he snapped for her to turn around. Lilo's slacks fell to his ankles and he roughly positioned Sydney the way he wanted her.

"Lilo!" Sydney protested.

"Shut up and bend over!" he snapped.
Sydney was slightly leaning instead of bending over as Lilo demanded, so he grabbed the back of her neck and forced her to bend over. He ordered her to

open herself for him like she was some cheap whore, Sydney felt.

"Open it!" Lilo ordered, applying pressure to the back of her neck.

Sydney reached back and did as he demanded and Lilo roughly handled her, causing her face to hit the mirror. When she tried to use one hand to brace herself, he made her use both her hands to accommodate his vicious battering. Sydney silently took Lilo's abuse for as long as she could—gritting her teeth, grunting and lifting herself to her toes.

The more Sydney tried not to respond, the more brutal Lilo became, battering her as if he paid for it, asking, "Who gave you this life? Who gave you this life?"

To make him hurry and stop, she shrieked, "You did! You did," bursting into tears.

She knew Lilo hadn't given her anything that she hadn't already accomplished, but she was too scared to defend herself. Lilo roughly snatched himself out of her and quickly turned her to face him. He wrapped her in his arms like she was the love of his life. Out of breath, he kissed her lips, inhaling through his nose. He gripped Sydney's body parts, calling her his sweet thang—smacking her backside before pulling away completely and pulling up his pants. A few days had pasts before Lilo explained his behavior. He promised everything that happened was stress-related, claiming he'd been going through moments of doubt about who was really with him, and who was with him for the right reasons. He insisted the slap that night was *only* because he truly thought she was about to bite him, and assured her that he would have never laid a hand on her like that for any other reason.

He further claimed the way he handled her in the bathroom was about marking his territory, "This guy you call your best friend bothers me," he said.

"But I told you he's harmless Lilo. I promise," Sydney admitted.

"Maybe…Maybe not. I don't know. But I can't see any man being your best friend and not falling in love with you. I know how much I love you," he claimed.
Lilo used the l-word and Sydney's heart begged for confirmation. She asked if he did for real or was, he just saying that.

"You know I do," he whispered.

"But you scared me so bad," Sydney confessed. "I didn't know what I did to make you treat me like this."
Lilo apologized with a kiss and a diamond bracelet, which reminded Sydney of the sweetness she fell for in the beginning. Immediately, she was able to

breathe again, until the day she met Barbara, Lilo's wife. Sydney arrived at the studio about half an hour earlier than scheduled. Sydney was playing the piano when Lilo's wife, Barbara showed up at the studio unexpectedly. Barbara had always steered clear of Lilo's exploits in order to protect their children but it was something about Lilo's new artist that drew Barbara out of her comfort zone. One look at Sydney in person and Barbara knew exactly why Lilo spent so much time with her. The made-up version of her on magazine covers didn't do any justice. The girl looked better in person. Barbara couldn't help comparing herself, especially after being in such a stressful marriage filled with infidelities. They'd taken a toll on her. The lines on her forehead seemed permanent, especially after introducing herself and getting straight to the point with her one-sided speech.

"It's exciting at first. Spending time with such a handsome and well-capable man can be enchanting. The lovemaking can be off the charts; perhaps the best you've ever had, being such a young girl. I suppose it can make you feel like you're in love...until you meet his wife," Barabara said, exuding sophistication.

Sydney's eyes darted from left to right, looking for Lilo or anyone else who could stop the impending scene from getting ugly. Lilo said he and his wife were separated and going through a divorce. He said she was living in New Jersey, so Sydney sat wondering why Mrs. Lilo was in Atlanta about to charge her up.

It didn't take rocket science to know silence was the best option, as Barbara continued, "You're young and I can understand how this has happened. That is not to say I'm giving you a pass, because I'm not. I'm just letting you know that you need to quit while you're ahead, because I don't want to have to come to this studio again. I'm sure you're smart enough to understand exactly what I mean by that," Barbara concluded, before turning to leave just as she came—sophisticated and calm.
Sydney could have slid underneath the piano in shame. Ten minutes afterwards, Lilo walks into the studio and Sydney was sure he'd run into his wife, because he was acting a little detached. She dared to ask him if his wife was the reason he seemed to ignore her, because his normal demeanor was body to body contact. His conversation was face to face, eye to eye. In the studio her kept her close; under his wing, especially around the musicians. He made sure everyone in close proximity knew she was off limits. Five minutes had passed and there was still at least five feet of distance between them. No touch. No

hug. No, come here baby, and her coming to him like a little puppy dog. Nothing. He just started laying out the details for the session.

'Ugh! Say something to me,' Sydney thought, as Lilo went on and on about how positive things were going with the album and how the lead single performed beyond expectation. He claimed he was almost ready to pull the trigger on the album release, but there was one thing he needed to change on track nine.

"The hook," he said.

"The hook?" Sydney asked, annoyed.

"Yeah, the hook. You got a problem with that?" he questioned.

"No…" Sydney replied, folding her arms.

"I didn't think so. But this is what I was thinking," he said as he began snapping his finger and patting his foot before singing the hook he wanted. Sydney thought his version sounded too country—Nashville country. When Lilo told Sydney to sing it, she sang it like it was recorded and Lilo corrected her nicely and told her to try it again. Sydney gave it to him again but with no conviction. Lilo demanded a little more.

Sydney looked at Lilo with deep frustration and in front of the whole production team, she had a meltdown, "I already gave you everything, and you just walk in here and don't even speak to me, don't touch me…just give me a damn hook and say sing. Really, Lilo?"

Lilo looked at Sydney as if she had lost her mind. He pointed at her and reminded her that she was in his session, "Never interrupt my session with personal business," he reminded.

"SCREW YOUR SESSION!" Sydney yelled, frustrated.

Complete silence ensued. Everyone was shocked, but no one moved. Lilo calmly ordered everyone to get out—except for Sydney, who stood there twisting her fingers like a nervous child. She prepared for a hug or some form of personal attention because she believed he loved her. Instead, she met a backhand of knuckles to the side of her head that sent her crashing to the floor—sliding.

Lilo's face twisted face as if he'd turned into another person again, "Don't you ever disrespect me! In case you forgot, this is my house. MINE!" Lilo replied, hitting his chest.

Once again Sydney was too horrified to move from her sprawled position. The pain on the side of Sydney's head grew gradually, but the lights she saw were still flickering in her right eye.

She burst into uncontrollable tears, "You said you wouldn't hit me again."

Lilo's face changed again and with tears in his eyes he reached to help her from the floor, "Come here baby. I'm sorry. I'm sorry, but I need you to trust me when it comes to my music. I've been doing this a long time and I know what I'm doing. I know what I'm doing," he repeated.
Sydney trembled like a leaf in Lilo's grasp and flinched every time he attempted to touch her face. He hugged her and kissed the side of her head, the place he'd hit. He continued apologizing, holding, hugging, and kissing her until she wiggled from his grasp and stepped back.

"Lilo, you told me you were getting a divorce," Sydney charged.

"I am baby."

"You said your wife lived in New Jersey," Sydney charged.

"She does," he defended.

"Then why was she here?" Sydney questioned.

"When?" Lilo asked as if he was concerned.

"C'mon Lilo. You know your wife was here today. You came in right after she left," Sydney informed.
Lilo denied knowing his wife had come to the studio but inquired why she came.

With a sudden burst of boldness, Sydney told him why she came, "She came to tell me to do just what I'm doing—leaving you alone!"
Sydney tried to walk away and in mid-step, Lilo snatched Sydney's arm—snatching her backward as if she'd been tied to a bungee cord.

"No Lilo!" Sydney screamed, ducking and covering her head, thinking he was about to beat her.

Lilo snatched Sydney like a rag doll to make her stand up, but Sydney kept struggling to keep her face covered, screaming, "Stop it Lilo! Stop it!" she begged.
Robert, the bass player, rushed into the studio and grabbed Lilo from behind, pleading for him to calm down. Lilo let her go and faced Robert in a rage. He blistered Robert with insults and fired him on the spot. Scared and desperately confused, Sydney stood in place nearly about to pee her pants until Lilo started to calm down. He ordered Sydney to go get herself cleaned so they could finish up, but when Sydney left Lilo's presence she bypassed the lady's room and rushed to her truck and left Solara. On the way, Sydney alternated between fighting tears and losing the fight. Eventually, she had to pull over to try to regain some composure, but her vision blurred and tension clamped her neck muscles like a vice grip. Anxiety filled her chest like a balloon and she

screamed to the top of her lungs as every image of being humiliated flooded her mind. She banged on the steering wheel and cussed Lilo aloud—calling him out of his name. Finally, she took in a deep breath and blew out, making a whining sound. She looked at her face in the rearview mirror. She looked different. Just a week ago her eyes were glowing but now they were wearing stress like designer shades. The puffiness from crying was horrible. She stroked the puffiness as if to iron it away but it stayed. When Sydney arrived at Pamela's, she told her what happened at the studio; painfully describing the emotional trauma of being talked to so disrespectfully and how Lilo had grabbed her arm, snatched on her, pointed his finger in her face, and yelled at her. Pamela scowled at Sydney's description of Lilo's behavior and asked if he'd ever reacted like that before.

Sydney denied he had but admitted they'd gotten into a few disagreements, "Just like in all relationships," Sydney claimed.
Pamela still called Lilo's actions excessive and unthinkable and suggested Sydney call the police, which had never crossed Sydney's mind.

"He was just angry," she explained.

Pamela assured Sydney that things would only get worse, "If he's yelling and grabbing on you right now, it's only a matter of time before he hits you," she assured.

Sydney felt Pamela's words in the pit of her stomach and knew she couldn't tell her the truth, and getting the police involved was out of the question. Sydney didn't want to go that far.

"He's gonna come looking for you…either at your place, the WCPA facility…or any other place you hang out. You should call the police," Pamela reasoned.

Sydney rejected Pamela's suggestion to call the police, and instead reached out to David. She called his mom, who tracked him down. She called Sydney back with David on a three-way call. He and Tomeka were at Astroworld and had just got in line for the Texas Cyclone.

"Anyway," Sydney interrupted. "Can you come and spend a few days with me…and still come for our birthdays?" Sydney requested.

"Yeah, but what's going on?" David questioned.

"Nothing…I just want you to come," she claimed.

"Ok," David answered, suspicious.

"Can you get on a plane tonight?" Sydney asked.

"Girl, no." David snapped, firing off excuses like he was throwing punches, *His mama would have a heart attack if he left suddenly like that. He didn't have anything packed. He needed to get some money together. He had to talk to Mr. Sammy first.*

Sydney waited for him to stop his whining and reminded him that his mama was on the three-way and that she knew she wanted him to come to Georgia.

"You know you don't need any money…you have that credit card. Plus, we can get you some things when you get here if we have to," Sydney claimed.

"Syd, I can't leave tonight," David replied.

"Well, can you do eleven-forty-five in the morning?" Sydney pushed.

David sighed, calculating the time, knowing he was spending the night in Houston, which meant he would have to leave Houston earlier than planned. He asked if there was a later flight.

"Two-*fifteen*," Sydney answered with frustration.

"Ok, I may be able to do that one," David settled.

"Are you sure?" Sydney questioned.

"Yeah, Knucklehead."

"OK, thank you Buckethead. I'll see you tomorrow."

BODY GUARD

Pamela waited patiently at the end of the walkway as the Continental flight passengers trickled off the plane. She looked for a caramel cutie in hard starched jeans, with a cocky walk and a dangerous smile. That's how Sydney described David. She even demonstrated his walk and told Pamela she wouldn't miss it. Three brothers with caramel skin passed Pamela but neither fit what Sydney described. One of them was with his girl and the other two were alone, but they were both sort of chunky. The fourth one approaching was wearing a blue wind-suit with an Astros baseball cap down to his eyebrows. He walked similar to how Sydney described, and as he passed her, he smiled. *Bingo,* Pamela thought.

"Excuse me, David?" Pamela asked.

"Well, that depends on who's asking," David answered, with a flirtatious smile.
Pamela extended her hand and introduced herself as Sydney's assistant.

"Well, hello Pamela…Sydney's assistant. But who says I'm David?"

"That dangerous smile Sydney described, and I would have to agree," Pamela admitted.

"Is that right? What else did this Sydney say about this David?"

"That you're a flirt and I would have to agree with that too," Pamela admitted, smiling.

David questioned, "How you figure?"

"Because you're still holding my hand."

"Well, that's because you're letting me," David replied.

"Ah Ahem…then can I have my hand back?"

"Sure, you can," David answered, allowing Pamela to retract her hand.

She told him to follow her and he did, but when she felt him checking out her goods, she corrected herself and told him to walk with her. After retrieving his bag, they went to Pamela's car, where Sydney was waiting in the driver's seat. As soon as Sydney saw Pamela and David, she crossed over to the passenger side instead of getting out and walking around. She motioned like an anxious child for David to hurry up to get in, and as soon as he did, she was on her knees in the front seat, reaching back for a hug. On the way to Sandy Springs to get Sydney's truck from Pamela's, David and Sydney talked as if they were alone. Pamela laughed at their childish antics—pushing and pinching each other, calling each other names, revealing their closeness. However, the silliness was mainly one-sided, exposing a side of Sydney that Pamela had not met. Sydney had been mostly composed and clear, but there she was, changing topics like she was flipping pages in a book. The look on David's face, as Pam glanced a few times in the rearview mirror, suggested he was wondering what was really going on. Sydney talked about her new townhome, how nice it was, and how thick the walls were. Then she took an unexpected turn and mentioned how she could get him inside and make him scream like a girl and no one would hear him. Pamela's eyes bucked, but she continued looking straight ahead as though she heard nothing.

"Yeah, right," David replied.

"Yeah right, nothing. You know how I make you do that lil squeal thang," she teased.
David smacked, annoyed.

"Boy don't play. You know want me to tie you up and abuse you."

David scowled, "Girl, that don't even sound right coming out of your mouth."
Sydney asked if it would sound better going into her mouth. Then she opened wide and laughed at her joke. David shook his head—agitated.

"Girl, what's going on with you? And don't say nuthin because I know you. What is it?" David questioned.

"Nothing," Sydney squeaked. "Seriously…"

"Aight," David answered, unconvinced.

After retrieving Sydney's truck and heading to her place, she drove, periodically touching David until deciding to interlock her fingers with his. The move signaled she was nervous about something, but David patiently waited for her to volunteer what was going on. When Sydney pulled into the swanky neighborhood, looking like she was expecting the unexpected. David's defenses were raised. It worsened when she pulled into her garage, but left the engine running until the garage door closed. Then she announced their arrival. They went inside, but Sydney still appeared to be a little anxious. David preoccupied himself with the plush furniture, polished wood, painted pictures, and other decorations. A quick tour of the place led right into Sydney's bedroom, which was equally impressive. It was set up as if it belonged at a resort. She had a king-sized bed with leather padding and thick linen coverings. The nightstands and lamps were wall-mounted, and the room had its own temperature control. It was freezing. Her walk-in closet was full of clothes—the racks bulged with garments and garment bags. The floor of the closet and the top rack were full of shoes—heels, sandals, and sneakers. David thought it was excessive. Sydney fidgeted and kept walking past David, nervously doing nothing, until he grabbed her from behind.

He hugged her about the shoulders with his face against hers, and asked, "What's wrong? Why are you so nervous?"

The side view of Sydney's face revealed that she wasn't exactly ready to talk. She was enjoying David's bear hug from the back, acting like she hadn't been hugged in a while. She exhaled, knowing she couldn't just blurt out what happened, so she decided to start with the threat from Lilo's wife. Sydney claimed Lilo had been pressing her for more than a business relationship, and that they sort of went there, but after the ordeal with his wife, Sydney claimed she broke it off and that Lilo was upset about that. She concluded by saying she and Lilo got into a nasty argument at the studio after she had broken off the relationship, and that it got so bad that she had to leave the studio in the middle of a session.

"Since I left, he's been calling my phone like crazy. It made me realize I didn't have anyone here besides Pamela, so I called you," Sydney confessed. Of all the information Sydney shared, David heard the one thing she didn't say—she was messing around with Kenny's cousin.

"This doesn't have anything to do with Kenny!" Sydney barked.

"Well, it don't sound like it has anything to do with me either," David snapped.

Sydney clenched her teeth, took in a deep breath, and blew, making her lips flap.

"David…all I need right now is my friend. Can you just be my friend? Please…"

They entered a staring contest with only a few blinks here and there until David agreed to give her what she asked for. That's when the doorbell rang and Sydney's heart skipped two beats. She hoped it wasn't Lilo because if it was, *Plan A* had just failed. She expected Lilo to call before he came. That would have allowed her to give David a heads-up but if that was Lilo at the door, *Plan B*, which wasn't a plan at all, would have to kick in by default. That meant throwing David into the ring—blind.

Sydney hopped off the bed and urged David to get the door for her. She wasn't sure if it was Lilo, but claimed, if it was, she didn't want to deal with him. That's when she realized she was afraid to deal with him. At first, she thought she was just confused and hurt, but she was shaking—terrified. She waited by the sofa in clear view, so Lilo could see her when David opened the door. David opened the door and Lilo prepared to barge in but was shocked to see a man. He froze with a look of confusion. He asked

David who the hell he might be, and David just stood there without answering.

"I'm here to see Tre´. Can you move? Can you move please?" Lilo requested.

David didn't move, but yelled for Sydney without taking his eyes off of Lilo. He asked if she wanted *this dude* to come in.

"No," she faintly answered.

David yelled for clarity, "What was that?"

Sydney repeated herself, except a little louder and David echoed her response, "She don't want to see you bruh."

"Well, let's get one thing straight. First of all, I ain't your bro," Lilo corrected. "And I don't give a damn what she wants…this is business and this is money. And this s—t y'all got going on here, is f—king with my money." Lilo pointed in Sydney's direction and threatened, "You better have your ass in the studio tomorrow or—"

"Or what nigga?" David barked. "Or what?" David defended.

"David don't!" Sydney yelled.

Lilo looked around for spectators and sort of laughed before squaring off, "Boy, you don't know who you're f—king with."

"Then show me," David challenged, planning to straight jab Lilo's chin any second.

Lilo backed away down the steps before turning and walking towards his black Ferrari. Instinct prompted David to step back into the house just in case Lilo had a gun, but he got into his car, started the engine, revved it a few times, and drove away calmly. David closed and locked the door—his adrenalin pumping. He exhaled, relieved that things didn't come to blows, but when he saw how frightened Sydney was, he wished he would have beaten the brakes off of Lilo. Sydney was quiet, but David could see the pulse in her neck and her upper chest from across the room. She was sweating and breathing through her mouth, and giving off a fragrance David hadn't smelled in years. It hit his nostrils like he'd been punched in the nose. The stench of fear and abuse seeped from Sydney's pores. She smelled just like his mama used to smell whenever Black had slapped, or abused her, and it turned David's stomach. He asked her if Lilo had put his hands on her, and before Sydney could answer, David warned her not to lie. Sydney denied Lilo had ever hit her, but David knew she was lying. He knew what abuse smelled like. He tenderly lifted Sydney's face and asked again, and again, Sydney said no—that she would never just let someone put their hands on her.

"Look…" David began. His voice was low and raspy. His eyes squinted—teary. "I don't care who it is. I don't care where it is…or even what for. If anybody…and I mean anybody…ever…put their hands on you, I want you to tell me. You hear me?" Sydney nodded, yes, but reached up to take David's hand from her right temple. It was still sore from Lilo's knuckles. She apologized for the confusion but thanked him for making her feel safe. The next morning Sydney went to the studio to finish the track the way Lilo wanted it. Lilo was still wearing his feelings but he managed to stick to business. He told Sydney what he wanted and once she did it, the session for her part of the project was complete. She came home and finished the week with David before he flew back to Houston—just in time for Rosalind's birthday. David and Rosalind spent the weekend together. Everything was Rosalind and David gave her his undivided attention. She was the main attraction, the main dish, the gourmet dessert—his sweet, chocolate pound cake. However, despite being treated like a queen, Rosalind still found a moment to lament being single. She attributed her singleness to what she referred to as three strikes— dark-skinned, intelligence, and professional.

She claimed most men prefer not to date smart, professional women. "And when you factor in dark skin, a sister might as well have leprosy," she claimed.

The very things Rosalind was calling strikes, were the very things David loved about her. For his kind words, she referred to him as an extreme exception to the *unwritten* rule—which was why she regrettably let herself sink as far as she did. With him, she knew she was experiencing everything she wanted in a relationship—from public affection to being greedily ravished throughout the night. Sex with him was blissful, though she admitted having sex with him was extremely selfish on her part. She confessed to know he would willingly do everything she needed him to do, which is what made her decision to break it off so hard. Rosalind claimed the only other thing that was harder than that moment of self-preservation, was looking Martie in the face, knowing what she'd been doing with her son behind her back. David thought break-ups were supposed to involve cussing and threats and promises that you never want to see that person again. However, lying there listening to Rosalind bring what they had to an end and why, was a whole new world. It caught him completely by surprise. She had performed a highly complicated surgery with such skill that David couldn't be upset. She explained her reasons for breaking up with such care and bowing out gracefully was because she had to. Competing with younger women didn't work for her. Competing with Ara alone had been hell.

"Just knowing you were getting out of Ara's bed on Saturday mornings and climbing into mine on Saturday evenings ate away at my dignity." She admitted that even then, getting off of the rollercoaster didn't become a serious option until he made plans to spend a whole month in Georgia with Sydney. "And even now, I'm regretfully letting go," yet, she thanked him for making her feel so special. On the flight back to Atlanta, David reflected heavily on Rosalind's words and how she ended their arrangement. No doubt, he was already missing their moments together, and letting go of the visuals of her body and facial expressions wasn't going to be easy. He'd fantasized about her since he was a child, and to finally get it—unexpectedly, was a private joy that exceeded all of his little freaky fantasies about her. *'But all good things must come to an end,'* he reasoned. David's flight landed at Hartsfield-Jackson at 2:30 PM. Pages from Sydney's home phone came through as soon as he turned on his pager. The last page included a 911 message but Pamela was already at the airport waiting for him. She explained Sydney was still tied up with the birthday planner and that she enlisted her at the last moment to rush over to get him. I-85 traffic was hectic in both directions, so

Pamela decided to take I-285 East. It was a little longer, but it bettered their chances of not being held up too long. It still took nearly two hours. It was 4:45 PM when Pamela turned onto Niblick Dr., and by then, Sydney was paging her too. As soon as Sydney saw Pamela's car pull up she opened the door all dramatic, swinging it wide open and whipping her honey-blonde permed hair. The girl looked like that Tuesday Taylor doll she had in the second grade.

"What took y'all so long?" she asked.

As Pamela was about to explain how crazy the traffic was, David grabbed Sydney's face and kissed her right on the lips, "Muah! Hello to you too…Tuesday Taylor."

"I paged you like five times Buckethead. And I paged you too," Sydney said to Pamela, sneering. Pamela attempted to explain again, but ignored her. She was too busy playfully bumping David with her hip as he was attempting to squeeze past her. As he made it past her, he gave her a quick pop on the butt that sounded like a hand clap. Pamela handed Sydney David's smaller bag and asked if she needed anything else. Sydney claimed she didn't, but invited Pamela to come inside. Pamela hesitated to accept the invite, because even though Sydney was smiling, her cattiness was in full effect. It wasn't the first, second, or third time she'd witnessed it.

Suddenly, a high-pitched squeal sounded and a voluptuous beauty appeared, excitedly skip-bouncing towards David with open arms.

"Hey, you!"

"Tasha?" David asked, surprised.

"Yes!" Tasha answered, crashing into David, putting his neck in a death lock, "Oh my god…I haven't seen you in like forever," she claimed, bouncing.

"Wow…look at you…all grown-up…and looking like a woman with them hips!" David teased.

"Yep! I got em from my mama," Tasha blushed. She hugged David again, "And no braids…I like…" Tasha admired, "Them waves got a sista seasick."

"Oh Lord…it's you," Lydia growled.

"Liddy!" David spoke, excited to see her. Lydia made a sick face and dry-heaved when David opened his arms and started in Lydia's direction.

Before David got within three feet of her, she turned and clammed up, telling Sydney, "Get it!" as if David was someone's house pet. David grabbed her in a bear hug and kissed her cheek, but she told him to move, calling him a pest.

"Oh, so, it's like that now?" David wondered.

"David, move…you know you get on my nerves," Lydia claimed.

"Why do I get on your nerves? I thought we were cool," David assumed.

"What on earth gave you that idea?" Lydia questioned.

"When you stayed at my apartment," he answered. "You ate my food…slept in *my* bed and now you wanna act funky? Come here," David demanded, squeezing tighter.

"Sydney…get him!" Lydia yelled, moving her face away from David's lips, claiming she didn't want the cooties.

David let go, but he promised Lydia he was going to catch her before the day was over and give her a real, good Dino kiss. Lydia cringed at the gross visual, but Tasha mused, embracing that reality anytime. She planned, and whether or not she could pull it off depended heavily on David's responses to her subtleties. She helped him with his bags, and while they unpacked to get him settled, she filled him in on her last eight years. Things had been pretty rough living with her grandmother in Baton Rouge.

Graduating high school without her mom being there was tough, "But I'm a sophomore at LSU now, majoring in Business. I was planning to pledge Delta

Sigma Theta, but Sydney offered to pay my tuition if I pledged AKA," Tasha informed.

"That sounds like a heck of a deal to me," David added.

Tasha reluctantly agreed, but the best part about Sydney's offer was graduating debt free. Other than that, Tasha's experience with the AKA's at LSU hadn't been cordial.

"Those *heffas* don't have *any* dealings with brown-skinned girls," Tasha claimed. "That's why I thought to pledge Delta in the first place."

"Xi Psi has brown-skinned girls," David recalled.

"That's what cousin Sydney said," Tasha confirmed, before changing the subject. She asked what he been up to.

David boasted of being pro and undefeated but admitted he hadn't made any real money.

He simulated a few jabs, "Ya boy just gotta knock a few more noses before that real money come through."

Tasha smiled, agreeing she believed David could hit pretty hard.

"Oh yeah…ya boy can bring it," David confirmed. "I don't be playin…"

"That's what my cousin says. She said you know how to hit that spot," Tasha flirted.

David pushed Tasha, "Girl…get out of here with that."

Tasha laughed, but she was serious. Sydney had told her a lot about him, which is why she thinks she had such a huge crush on him back then. *'And now,'* she thought.

Again, David nudged her with his shoulder and told her to stop, "Sydney shouldn't have been telling you anything like that. You were just eleven years old."

Tasha chuckled and bumped David with her hip, "It's not like she was graphic. She just told me how you made her feel."

David bumped Tasha back and she exaggerated being knocked off balance—leaning away from him and catching herself against the headboard. She stood close to him; her hip touching his, and he didn't move. She counted that as a point. David asked if she had a boyfriend. She counted his interest as another point.

Tasha smacked her lips and replied, "I only have friends. Then again, I have a part-time friend. Sort of a friend. Actually, I don't really know what to call it. We just hookup whenever…and that's about it. Most guys don't want all of this," she criticized.

"All of what?" David questioned. "Do you think you're fat or something?"

"Well, whatchu call it?" Tasha asked.

"Fine. Thick. Voluptuously delicious," David answered, laughing.

Tasha's stomach fluttered—another point. She asked if he really thought so, and David assured her it was exactly what he thought. She went for the commitment, and asked him if he would get with a fine, thick, and voluptuously delicious girl like her.

"Hell Yeah…because you have shape to your thickness. I've always found that attractive," David expressed.

Tasha's smile stretched wide—showing all of her teeth. She thanked him, but before she could squeeze another compliment out of him, screams and laughter downstairs signaled the arrival of Sydney's sorority crew. Tasha gave David a fist bump, before heading downstairs to meet her future sisters.

GIRLS JUST WANNA HAVE FUN

Tasha's future sorority sisters were flipping their hair and talking cat-talk when she made it downstairs, and the first thing she noticed was that there was color in the house. There were three brown-skinned girls, one little-skinned girl—closer to Sydney's color and two *high*-yellow ones, gassing themselves up with that high-pitched screech. They gave each other delicate hugs and exaggerated kisses on each cheek—Muah. Muah. The ladies chanted some little chant, suggesting all the popular fraternities were chasing them. Tasha recalled that the AKA's at LSU weren't just chased—they were hunted. Guys on campus craved those light, bright, and almost white sisters. For some, it was like having the best of both worlds—the body of a sister with the color of another. The guys called them, *Face Pies.* Tasha snarled when David came downstairs acting no different than the guys she knew; like he was top dog in a room full of b—ches in heat. He was lost. He didn't even know what was going on. *Just trying to get some attention'* Tasha felt. She was completely turned off by the way he played himself, walking straight to Sydney like a little trained puppy—waiting to be introduced. She finally introduced him as her best friend from back home.

The ladies spoke, and Sydney introduced them, pointing as she called their names, "Aja, Dominique, Tammy, Raelyn, Sabrina…and my big *sister*…Marjorie."

Tasha snarled again at David's reaction, looking at Marjorie like she was candy dripping from a stick. At first impression, David judged Marjorie as the best-looking of all of Sydney's sisters. She wasn't as shapely as the others. She was slim-fine, with a huge gap and very impressive breasts. Marjorie was the only one who greeted David with a handshake, claiming she remembered seeing him on campus that one time, right before she graduated.

"You came to visit that little dark-skinned chick," she said.

"Tina," David corrected.

Marjorie sarcastically apologized, subtly dissing him, but David smiled, because the way she did it was cute. It looked like something his mom would have done. Judging shapes, Aja was unquestionably the finest of the group with dangerous curves. Tammy—coke bottle. Raelyn—hourglass. Dominique—amazon. Sabrina—Damn. Pamela wasn't one of them, but she was holding her own. She filled the image of the one who would most likely be in a meaningful relationship, while the others looked like they played games. In attitude, every one of Sydney's Sorors sucked except for Marjorie, who was laid back—cool and sexy. The others were just full of themselves—already talking about their exploits,

"You know how we do…We step in the place like…And every skeezer look at us like…And they better keep their dogs on a leash…" "Cuz a hungry dog will get fed!" Tammy bragged.

It only got a little more sickening when Sydney joined in, flipping her hair, talking loudly, and giving David his first-ever glimpse of *college girl* Sydney. She was gassed up too, but Lydia had enough and excused herself. David would have left to, but the entire room was swirling with fragrances of citrus, candy, and flowers, and nothing stimulated his senses like a fine, pretty woman, smelling mouthwatering delicious—except a room full of fine, pretty women, smelling mouthwatering delicious. The ladies put plans in the atmosphere. Marjorie wanted drinks. Everyone else wanted to eat. Dominique wanted both and some male company. David wanted the eggs and rice with bacon, just like Sydney promised him. She shushed him, giving him the eye, because none of her Sorors even knew she could cook. David insisted, wanting what he wanted, and was not going to let Sydney get out of it. It also gave him a chance to embarrass her a little by bragging on how good of a cook she actually was. His bragging set her apart, because none of her Sorors cooked, but was now suddenly interested in Sydney cooking. Sydney deflected, saying she might cook for them one day, but that day, she suggested they all go to the Tavern—a little swanky hangout not far from the village. Sports figures and some entertainers were known to come through from time to time, but mostly it was everyday good people. Sydney's face was familiar in the Tavern. She'd been there a few times, made some acquaintances, and had a picture with fans on the wall. Marjorie was a familiar face in the place too. She accepted a few hugs from guys but appeared cautious and distant with other females. Everyone sat in small groups, as close as possible. Sydney, Lydia, Marjorie, and Pamela sat together. David, Tasha, Dominique, and Sabrina sat together. Aja, Tammy, and Raelyn sat together, and after everyone got settled, the hungry folks ordered chicken and shrimp skewers, oysters on a half-shell, and fried calamari. The social drinkers, Raelyn, Aja, Tasha, and Pamela ordered Tom Collins and cherry margaritas.

Sydney, Tammy, and Sabrina ordered what they called, *inexperienced* mango daiquiris, saying together, that the daiquiris were no longer virgins, "But it's still tight," they said, giving each other high-fives.

Marjorie claimed hers was still tight too, but she ordered tequila shots and invited David to shoot with her. Remembering what happened the last time he shot tequila made it easy to pass on the invite. He ordered a corona—mainly for table decoration.

Dominique ordered tequila shots. She said hers wasn't tight. It was wild and loose, and anyone who came bumping against it had better bring the pain, "Because this heffa right here be kicking ass and taking names," she said, opening and closing her legs.

All the AKA's burst into laughter and gave each other hi-fives for the apparent inside joke. Tasha and David looked at each other and burst into a fake laugh, mocking, acting like they had their own inside joke. Sydney gave both of them the finger, by touching the tip of her nose with her middle finger. During the first round of drinks, Sydney and her sisters had a lot to laugh and talk about. They reminisced, reminding each other of things that happened back at A&M, and Sydney laughed so hard at some of those things until her face was red. It was obvious, she had a lot of fun in college. After a few more drinks, that neither of the ladies had to pay for, they stopped being so stuck-up. All of them, except Dominique, were starting to chill. It turned out, that Dominique was the silly one in the group. She got

David's attention and the two hit it off—talking trash to one another. They playfully dissed each other and debated about the most trivial and meaningless stuff—making up stuff. Dominique was also the most aggressive of the group. Her aggression seemed to increase with every sip. She was already teetering on inappropriate flirting with strangers who bought drinks, but then it was like someone flipped her switch and that playfulness between her and David went to another place. She told David that he needed to come and sit his fine ass down next to her so she could tell him something, and like a dodo bird, he went. Whatever Dominique whispered in his ear shocked the heck out of him—his eyes almost popped out of his head. Tasha read David's lips when he told Dominique, no, and she read Dominique's lips asking David, why not. She couldn't make out or hear David's explanation because whatever he was saying to Dominique, he was saying it directly in her ear. Then David's body jerked suddenly. Tasha was sure Dominique touched David under the table. At first, he played it off like nothing happened, but he looked like he'd been violated. Dominique looked like she was calming down while Daid was whispering in her ear, but Tasha wanted to invite her to a meeting in the ladies' room. Sydney sat there acting like she didn't see what happened, but it was because she was getting plenty of attention herself.

In the Tavern parking lot, Sydney extended an invitation to stay at her place—especially Marjorie, since she lived thirty minutes away. Marjorie was zooted but insisted she was cool, but when David asked her to stay, she accepted. It was eleven-thirty when the group flowed into Sydney's apartment, still talking and laughing about those crazy conversations at the Tavern. David mocked Dominique, saying the girl had problems. Sydney admitted she did, but didn't volunteer any details until she went to his room later. He was in the shower. Sydney perched herself on the sink before resuming their conversation about Dominique.

David called her, a trip, and Sydney admitted, "Yeah, she can be, but Dom's aggressiveness is front. She's a big teddy bear, with a soft heart."

"Shid…that girl acts like she will beat somebody down," David assessed.

"Oh, don't get me wrong, she'll fight," Sydney confirmed. "But she's a sucker for love. She likes you."

"Really?" David questioned.

Sydney smacked her lips, "Boy…you know she does. I saw her trying to get with you."

David denied Dominique was trying to get with him, but Sydney insisted she was right because she knew Dominique well. She interrogated, asking him what Dominique was talking about.

"You don't want to know that," David answered.

"Try me," Sydney dared.

David burst into laughter when he reflected on that conversation. He stepped out of the shower and admitted Domonique didn't say anything about him and her, "She was talking about me, and you. You heard us cutting up before she told me to come over to her, right?"

"Actually, she said bring your fine ass over her," Sydney corrected.

"Anyway! When I sat down, this girl looked me in my face and said, *I beat you be f—king the sh-- out of Sydney huh?*"

"WHAT?" Sydney snapped. "No, she didn't!"

"Yes, she did. And I was like, no girl…and she was like, *why not?* I explained to her that we were just friends, and that's when she said I couldn't just be her friend."

"Like I said…she was trying to get with you," Sydney insisted. "And you made quite an impression on Aja and Sabrina too. They both think you're a nice catch."

"Yea? And Marjorie?" David wondered.

"What about her?" Sydney questioned.

"What does she think?" David asked.

"Do you want me to tell you what I think?" Sydney replied

"What's that?"

"I think you need to know that all of my sisters, friends, and associates—past, present, and future are off limits. Do you understand mister man?" Sydney warned.

David laughed and Sydney mocked him, "Ha, ha, ha my ass. You don't make enough money for Marjorie anyway," Sydney informed.

"Is that what she—"

"ANY…way!" Sydney interrupted, "It felt good seeing you cut up tonight. It actually reminded me of how we used to cut up when you lived with us. Remember that?"

"Yeah, buddy. We used to cut up…bad," David remembered.
Sydney reminisced how comfortable it felt having him sleep in the next room over. She admitted how she fantasized about him creeping into her room just to lay in bed with her.

David laughed because he couldn't count the times he fantasized about creeping into her room back then, "But it *sho* wasn't just to lay in the bed. Man…if washcloths could talk," David confessed.

"Quit lying!" Sydney teased, "You were not choking your chicken next door!"

"Girl, I was strangling that chicken! PA-KURK!" Sydney burst into laughter; clapping her hands and kicking her feet, admitting David was not by himself in that regard, but that most of the time, she did only think about them lying in bed together.

"Like twins," she said.

David finished drying off and knowing his routine, Sydney handed David his jar of cocoa butter and watched him adequately moisturize himself before putting on his boxers.

"Turn around, let me get your back for you," Sydney offered.

When she finished moisturizing David's back, she hugged him from behind, kissed him on the cheek, and told him goodnight. It was five o'clock in the morning when David woke up from a confusing dream. He dreamt he and Sydney were in the kitchen preparing a meal together. She told him to close his eyes, that she had a surprise for him, and when he did, he felt a pain in the center of his chest. He opened his eyes and Sydney wasn't there. He looked at his chest and saw a gaping wound—a black hole and on the floor, a blood trail leading out of the kitchen. He followed it. It led to the front door, which was still open. When he made it to the front door, he looked outside and saw Sydney standing at the curb looking at him. She was holding his beating heart in one hand and a bloody butcher knife in the other.

David's eyes were wide open when Sydney walked into his room. She came in to let him know she was leaving for track practice and that Lydia was going with her. The other ladies would leave whenever they woke up, but she playfully warned him not to get too excited about being in the house full of women while she was gone. She didn't know how long it would be before she made it back, but she knew it would be after lunch.

"Just call my truck phone if you and Tasha leave," she requested.

Sydney looked so innocent and pretty with her big eyes, thick lips, and crooked smile. David just stared at her while she talked, until she playfully threatened that if he didn't stop looking at her the way he was looking, she would have to close the door and rough him up right quick. Perplexed by the dream, an early morning bang session was the furthest thing from David's mind. Sydney kissed him on the forehead and thanked him again for coming.

She expressed how much his being there meant to her, "It reminds me of how close we were. It's hard to explain, but it feels good," she said, before leaving the room.

It was 6:15 AM when Sydney arrived at the Region 3 private facility, and seeing the facility was the only thing that gave David's name a break. The whole ride over, except for the first ten minutes, Lydia unloaded her feelings about him. She was severely irked by everything David said or did. She had a problem with him looking at her, and even the way he carried on with Dominique, and for the most part, David didn't even realize he was irking her.

It was non-stop, but in mid-sentence, upon seeing the facility, Lydia's tune changed, "Wow! This is nice. It makes our facility look like a public park." Lydia's league, The International Association of Track and Field Professionals (IATFP), only had one track, which was recently upgraded from red gravel. Region 3 had three types of tracks, including an indoor track. They got out of the truck, and the transformation Lydia observed in Sydney was immediate. It was like she turned into another person. Everything Lydia had unloaded on the way there seemed to have vanished, as well as Sydney's newly developing R&B persona. The girl even walked differently. It reminded Lydia of the first time she met Sydney—that cocky freshman at A&M. Sydney approached the track as if she was going to battle—strong and proud. Her shoulders appeared more squared in her midriff top, and her legs and butt looked perfectly sculptured in her white running pants. During her warm-ups, her facial expressions were stone-faced and focused. She looked fierce. Sydney's coach, Willie Masters, a handsome middle-aged man, was a track and field genius. He knew everything about Sydney. He knew when to push her and when to ignore her. He knew when she held back and when she chopped her steps during her stride. He even knew the exact number of times her feet hit the track in both the one-hundred and two-hundred meters. He knew her like the back of his hand. Whatever he asked for, Sydney gave her best to give it with no complaints. At the same time, Coach Masters was dedicated to Sydney—no distractions. Lydia was near, but he never acknowledged her presence. He only spoke with his assistant, who checked off items on a clipboard and made notes. As soon as Sydney finished, her heart rate and blood pressure was checked, and she and Coach Masters walked a lap together, talking. When they made it back to the starting point, Sydney formally introduced them, though she had already informed him she was bringing a personal friend and fellow Olympian. There was something captivating about Coach Masters. Lydia felt it. He was strong, confident and knew what he was doing—no guessing games. He was a former sprinter and very astute in kinetics.

He complimented, "You're a helluva quarter horse. Have you considered the two-hundred, yet?" Lydia confessed that she'd been recently working at the two hundred, and planned to run it at her next meet. He asked her best time in the four-hundred,

"48.60," Lydia replied.

Coach Masters nodded with a smile, "That's good."

He attempted to mention the world record holder in the four hundred, but Lydia replied before he could get it out, "Marita Koch, 47.60"

"Officially," Coach answered with a smile, before launching into a story about a little black girl from Alabama named Evelina Kennedy. "Evelina was a walk-on at Grambling State University in the spring of 1978. I'd been coaching there for two years. There was nothing about this girl that said she could run. She was a chemistry major, but she wanted to run. The first time I timed this girl in the quarter, she ran 47.8. I thought something was wrong with my stopwatch. So, I timed her again after she caught her breath and she ran a 48.7. Two weeks before her first track meet, that young lady ran a 47.32."

"What?" Lydia gasped.

"Yes," Coach nodded. "She sure did."

"Wow. And how did she do in the track meet?"

"She never got her chance to compete. She and her boyfriend got into a terrible car wreck one week before the meet. Her leg was severely damaged. The young man didn't make it."

"Wow, that is so tragic…but a 47.32?"

"Yes," Coach assured. "I timed her personally."

"Where is she now?" Lydia questioned.

Coach Masters called to his assistant, who walked over to where they were standing.

He introduced her, "Lydia Moore, meet the unofficial four-hundred-meter world record holder…Evelina Kennedy-Masters."

Asking Evelina about her secret to a 47.32 time was natural, but Evelina didn't have a secret except for being able to maintain speed all the way through. She ran the quarter the same way a person would run a two hundred. Before that day, Evelina confirmed she had never run track, and that she'd come from a line of women academicians. So, trying out for track was her first act of rebellion against her mom. The unique friendship between Coach Masters and Evelina revealed itself through their laughing about the day they met. Upon seeing the little girl wanting to try out for the team, Coach thought the easiest way to get rid of her was to tell her to run around the track once, as fast as she could. He laughed, admitting he was planning on having a good laugh at seeing Evelina run out of gas, but the joke was on him.

"And I didn't know any better. I just ran as fast as I could, and had no idea if what I did was good or bad," Evelina admitted.

After the laughs, Evelina began sharing about the accident, and what coach Masters had done for her during recovery. He was there every step of the way, and that they'd been close ever since. Sydney returned from the shower wearing black and pink running pants, fluorescent pink sneakers, and a hot pink fitted shirt—all by Streak. She hugged Evelina first, and then Coach Masters. As Sydney and Lydia were leaving, coach reminded Sydney to stick to her diet.

She promised she would but mumbled under her breath about how hungry she was, "We're going to eat right now," Sydney whispered through clenched teeth and a fake smile.

As soon as they got into the truck, Sydney checked for missed calls. There was one from Lilo. She called home and no one answered the phone.

She poked out her bottom lip, "Hmph. I told Buckethead to call me if they left."

Lydia gave Sydney the side-eye, "You sure they left? They just might not be answering the phone."

"Shush you," Sydney ordered.

"Shush me nothing. You already know how I feel about that whole little thing they have going on. David is entirely too—"

"Liddy! Stop it," Sydney warned.

"No!" Lydia snapped. "You need to stop acting like you don't see what I see."

Sydney blew, making her lips flap, "Liddy, why do you have your pitchfork so far up David's behind? What has he done to you?" she asked.

"Nothing. But it's not me who I'm concerned about," Lydia confessed.

"And what does that mean?" Sydney asked, frustrated.

"It means, I'm concerned about you. You're falling again," Lydia accused.
Sydney put the truck in gear and pulled off, determined to keep Lydia from plucking her nerves.

"Sydney, when you get like this, you just…I don't know…it's like you willfully blind yourself. It's like you put so much trust in David and he's no different than any other guy who's hurt you. I mean, the way he and Dominique were carrying on last night was just…inappropriate…and you acted like you didn't see any of it. Not to mention the way he's always hugging and kissing on Tasha…I mean, c'mon…they act like they're together or something. They could be screwing right now," Lydia supposed. Sydney hadn't even made it out of the parking lot before she had to pull over and put the truck in park. It took a few seconds for her to catch her breath—to relax and to breathe. She took off her seatbelt and turned in her seat to face Lydia. She sat speechless for a moment—before asking Lydia why would she say such a thing to her. Lydia apologized, claiming she didn't mean to be harsh, but that she just wanted Sydney to pay attention to signs.

"Liddy! Tasha is like our little sister—" Sydney attempted to explain.

"Who is a grown woman!" Lydia interjected. "And a lot of *woman* at that. I know she's your cousin, and I know how you feel about her, but she's not a little girl Sydney. I know you see how she's all up under him, and him kissing her on the temple. You do know what temple kisses mean right?" Lydia questioned.

Sydney sighed and shook her head as if she was trying to shake visuals out of her mind. She defended David, saying he's always been that way. "He's that way with me. He's that way with his mom. He's that way with my mom. That's just him. And if you weren't being so mean to him, he would be doing the same to you. David is just affectionate like that," Sydney claimed.

"So, he smooches with your mom like that?" Lydia asked, cynically.

"It's not smooching Liddy. Believe me…I know when he's smooching," Lydia promised.

"I'm sure you do," Lydia replied.

"Liddy, what is it? Is this jealousy, or are you just being mean?"

"Sydney, I am not jealous of David…okay…and this is not about me."

"Yeah, right," Sydney growled.

"Hold up," Lydia cautioned. "Let's get one thing straight. I am who I am. Okay? I told you years ago how I felt about you…and that hasn't changed. I just don't try to force your feelings. I enjoy being your friend. I love you. I respect you, and I care about what happens to you. I know how you can get with David…I've seen it too many times and I'm telling you, he's no different than the rest of these dogs."

"So, it's all men?" Sydney asked.

"All the ones I've me," Lydia snapped.

Sydney turned her face away from Lydia, and Lydia reached over and made Sydney look at her again, "The first day I laid eyes on you, you were crying. I found out later that you were crying because of David. That was my introduction to

David. That's how you introduced him to me. Do you remember why you were crying? You were crying because you had an abortion. Why? Because he kicked you to the curb. Isn't that what you told me?" Lydia questioned, harshly, "So no, I'm not jealous of him, because I would have never done you like that."

Sydney clinched her jaws in disbelief, that Lydia would reopen that wound. She sighed, "Liddy, David is my best friend.'

"I thought I was your best friend too," Lydia challenged.

"You are Liddy."

"Then act like I'm important. Act like my feelings matter, Sydney. Humor me at least."

"Liddy! You are my friend…and when I tell you, you know things that I have never told David…believe it. I never told David about the abortion. I'm not sure if I ever will. I never told him what my uncle did to me…and for good reasons. I never told him the real reason me and Kenny broke up, because had I told him Kenny hit me, David would have beat the living daylights out of him," Sydney claimed.

"No, Sydney! Call it what it is," Lydia demanded.

"What?" Sydney asked, confused.

"Kenny did not just hit you. Call it what it is," Lydia argued.

Immediately, Sydney looked away and Lydia jerked her face towards her again, "Sydney! If you don't call it what it is, you'll keep making excuses every time it happens …now say it! Say it!" She demanded, "He beat your ass…and you were too afraid to report it! Now say it!"

"He did not—"

"Sydney! I know what I saw when I walked into that room! And had I not jumped on him myself he would have hurt you! Now don't do this to yourself…Say it!"

"Ok, Liddy! He beat me…alright? God!" Sydney grieved.

Lydia grabbed Sydney's hand and held it against her chest, "Look, baby…from the moment I realized how special you are, I carried you right here…In my heart," Lydia confessed. "All I ever want for you is for you to be happy…even if I'm not the one to make you happy. I want to see you have everything you deserve. I promise. And even if you decide to try this life with someone else, well, I can't lie, I would be devastated, which means you will never, ever be able to do this life in peace, because I will never, ever let you live it down. We can be a hundred years old and in wheelchairs and if I see you, I will push your old ass over," Lydia seriously joked.

They both burst into laughter, wiping their tears, but after a moment, Lydia asked Sydney if she loved David.

"You know I love him, Liddy."

"Then why aren't you with him Sydney?

"I don't know. It's not just one thing. Sometimes what I feel for David scares me. He has a way of making me feel like I have no control and it drives me crazy. I hate it. But then again, he's always been so many different things in my life at different times—my brother, my best friend…and no, it's not all about sex with us either. It's been a while since we were together like that. The last time he was here all we did was chill. He slept in my bed and we didn't do anything—just like old friends."

Lydia accepted Sydney's explanation, but admitted she still wasn't convinced David could be trusted. She bet Sydney if she went home unexpectedly, she would be surprised.

"Try it," Lydia challenged.

"Ok," Sydney agreed, "But we're going to eat first. I'm starving."

LET'S MAKE IT HAPPEN

David came in from his jog and yelled he was back, before trotting upstairs.

Tasha rushed out of the kitchen just in time to catch a whiff of *sweaty man* fragrance, "Mmmm…" She admired. "Are you hungry?" She yelled.

David yelled back, "Yea! Let me shower first." Tasha heard what David said, but decided she didn't hear him at all. She went to his room to ask again, but his door was closed. She stood quietly outside of his door, listening, she could hear the radio, *'Every Little Step,'* by Bobby Brown was on. David was singing. He didn't sound too bad, but Tasha held in her laugh, wondering if David was in there dancing too. She lightly tapped on the door before opening it slowly, widening her eyes to peek in—hoping to get a glimpse of him in the buff. He was already in the bathroom. She could hear the shower. She crept in, looking around as if she were in his room for the first time. David's sweaty t-shirt was across the arm of the chair and his ankle socks were on the floor next to his sneakers. Tasha looked around for his sweaty shorts and maybe his jock strap too, but neither were in the room. She figured he must have taken them off in the bathroom. She nervously grabbed David's sweaty t-shirt and buried her nose in it. His man fragrance gave her chills and caused her to squeeze her thick thighs together. Her breath trembled when she exhaled. Listening to the changing sound of the shower, Tasha visualized the water traveling over David's fine body. Deviously, she thought about getting butt naked and walking into the bathroom. The voice in her head dared her to do it. Her heart was pounding as she loosened the string on her shorts. She lowered them all the way down to her thighs before stopping and doubting herself. She pulled them up again, before wondering if she was just punking out. Once again, she lowered her shorts once, but when she heard the shower stop, she quickly snatched them up again. She tried to tip out of the room but her sandal popped against her heel and David heard it.

"Tasha?" David called from the bathroom. Tasha froze and realized she still had David's sweaty t-shirt in her hand. She tossed it towards the chair but it fell short. David abruptly came out of the bathroom with a towel wrapped around his waist and saw Tasha standing at the bedroom door. She nervously asked again if he wanted to eat breakfast. She claimed she wasn't sure if he heard her ask him when he first came in. He told her yes, he was hungry.

"I have biscuits, eggs and sausage already, but I can do you some pancakes if you like," she offered.

"Biscuits is cool, but I like my eggs scrambled soft," David replied.
Flirtatiously, Tasha asked if he meant soft like her, to which David, responded yes. His devilish grin drew Tasha. She flirted more, asking what else was hiding behind the door. She moved towards the foot of the bed, bringing a little more of David's half-hidden body into view. He just stood there while Tasha admired his wet skin and the nice curve in the front of that towel.

***

Sydney and Lydia were leaving Le Tudor Bistro, just as Rich, a music producer and friend of Marjorie's, approached. Rumors had traveled fast. He claimed he heard Sydney was leaving Solara Records, but Sydney corrected that information. She told him everything was fine between her and Solara Records.

Rich corrected his information, "Actually, I heard you were not getting along with Lilo. I heard you guys are having some artistic conflicts."
Sydney didn't deny or confirm. She just looked at Rich, trying not to pay too much attention to his high, high-top fade. Rich gave a quick spiel about what he had going on. Seemingly, in one breath, he

mentioned having a few hot artists he'd been working with and the few he'd signed to his label. He also mentioned having some material that her voice was made for.

"Why don't both of you come to my party tonight, and you and I can talk about what I have…let you hear some things," Rich suggested.

Sydney blushed, "I don't know. Marjorie told me your last party was pretty wild."
Rich didn't deny the claim, but promised the party that night would be more laid back. He said it was set up to be more of a meet and mingle, with a little something for everybody. He insisted they come, but Sydney wasn't sure, it wasn't just her and Lydia. Her best friend and cousin were in town also.

"Friend, friend or friend…friend?" Rich asked.

"Oh, he's my best friend from childhood…more like my brother," Sydney answered.

Lydia felt like she could have puked in her mouth, but Rich laughed and told Sydney she could bring her friend, who is more like a brother. Lydia decided she had enough of Sydney's flirt and dance routine. She walked away, mumbling, calling Sydney a flirtmonger and a floozy, and criticized Rich's Kid n Play haircut. In the truck, Sydney admitted she didn't like Rich's haircut either but that she did think he was cute. As she prepared to drive away, she saw

Lilo walking towards her truck. He was dressed in workout gear—a tank top, biker shorts, and sneakers. He went to Sydney's driver side window and asked her to lower the glass. She did but brashly told him that she would see him at the meeting in a few hours.

Lilo arrogantly insinuated that Sydney apparently wanted to see him then, "Why else would you be at our favorite café on our day of the week?" he asked, cynically.

Sydney sighed in disgust. Lilo smirked. He asked her to look at him and she did. He asked if they could get past the drama and Sydney couldn't answer. He claimed he wanted to get past it, and that he would rather be making beautiful music with her. That was his way of saying he wanted to make love to her, because that's what they used to do after brunch. When Sydney didn't reply, Lilo reached in to caress her chin but she flinched. She regained her composure, hoping Lydia didn't notice, but how could she not? The flinch wasn't exactly subtle. Lilo said he was flying out to Los Angeles later that night, and that he would be there for a few days. He hinted that it would be nice to have some company.

"I'm sure you won't have a problem with that," Sydney answered.

Lilo chuckled, "I love you too."

Sydney smacked her lips and drove off.

Lydia dry-heaved, acting like she puked in her mouth again, "Ewww…hairy arms. Hairy legs. I hate hairy men," Lydia claimed, "Hairy chest. Hairy back. Hairy balls," Lydia gagged, again.

Sydney interrupted Lydia's moment of drama, assuring her that all guys have hairy balls.

"I wouldn't know," Lydia claimed, "I didn't see any hairy balls."

Sydney laughed and challenged, "Oh, you've seen some hairy balls."
Defensively, Lydia denied such an experience. Sydney called the names of two hot guys she remembered Lydia going out with back in college, and again, Lydia denied seeing hairy balls. She swore those guys couldn't even prove she was a woman, because nothing happened.

Sydney purposely agitated her, "Liddy, you didn't give nobody the business?"

"Oh, I gave somebody the business, but I didn't see no hairy balls."
It was eleven-forty-five when Sydney turned onto Niblick Dr. Instead of pulling into the garage, she parked out front as Lydia had recommended. She nervously prepared herself as best she could. They were both going to go inside, but at the last moment, Sydney asked Lydia if she would stay put and wait

for her. Lydia agreed, but pleaded for Sydney not to get herself in trouble if the worst was true. Sydney promised, hoping everything she was feeling was wrong. Before opening the front door, Sydney paused and looked back at Lydia, who urged her with her eyes to go inside. Sydney quietly entered her house—eyes wide, nose flared and heart pounding. She was hoping like crazy Lydia was wrong in her assumptions, but the horrific images she'd painted in her mind were fearful. Sydney scanned the main area as she by-passed her room and softly trotted upstairs. She walked into David's room and startled Tasha prancing out of David's bathroom, wearing only a jersey. With a razor-sharp tongue, Sydney asked Tasha what the hell was she doing in David's room. Tasha answered, almost stuttering, that she just finished showering.

"Why?" Sydney asked, as she abruptly walked past Tasha to look into the bathroom for David.

"Because…I wanted to take a shower," Tasha answered.

"So, why are you in here?" Sydney snapped.

"What's going on with you?" Tasha snarled. "I just told you why?"
Sydney bucked her eyes, waiting on an answer.

Tasha bucked her eyes back at Sydney, "I don't know what else you want me to say. I asked David if I can use his shower, and I used the shower."

"Why didn't you just use my shower?" Sydney investigated.

"Because David is in your bed," Tasha explained, annoyed.

"My bed?"

"Yes…he went and laid down in your bed after we ate breakfast," Tasha explained. "Since he was in there, I asked if it was ok to use his shower. BECAUSE…I wanted to take a shower and not a bath."

Sydney didn't immediately respond, but hearing David was in her bed felt like a ton of bricks had just tumbled out of her head—relief. However, it only made room for another question. Sydney asked Tasha why she was wearing David's favorite basketball jersey with nothing on underneath it.

"Cousin Sydney!" Tasha snapped in frustration, "David gave me the damn jersey because I told him Iceman Gervin is my favorite basketball player." She lifted the jersey, "And I have on a thong." Tasha fixed her hands like claws and hissed at Sydney like an angry cat, mocking Sydney's demeanor. Tasha asked again what was going on with her. With less defensiveness, Sydney explained she was upset with Lilo, and that seeing her when she was expecting to see David, caught her off guard.

"Um hmm…if you ask me, I think somebody's in heat," Tasha remarked.

"Well, ain't nobody asking you," Sydney replied, before heading downstairs to her room.

The moment Sydney saw David lying in her bed, in her spot, the havoc Lydia's voice had wreaked in her mind was finally silenced. She climbed into the bed and joined him looking at the ceiling. She exhaled. David asked what was wrong but Sydney shook her head, nothing. Then she admitted she was tired and still had to go to Atlanta for a meeting at the label.

After a few moments of silence, Lydia appeared in the doorway reminding Sydney of the time, "You're going to be late."

"I'm coming. I'm coming," Sydney answered.

"Wait for me, I'm about to come witchu," David said.

"You coming?" Sydney asked.

"Yeah, I'm almost there," David answered, smiling.

Sydney screamed in laughter when she picked up on David's joke.

Lydia snarled, "Eww…you are such a perv."

Sydney continued laughing like that was the funniest thing she'd heard all day, and the more she laughed the more Lydia was irked by their sick sense of humor. Even after they got into the truck, Sydney was still tickled. Despite Lydia being slightly disconnected the whole ride, Sydney realized David's joking with her was needed. It helped her nervousness and for one of those strange and unexplainable reasons, it made Sydney feel like everything was going to be alright. It was one o'clock on the nose when Sydney pulled into Solara's private driveway. Lydia's eyes lit up when she saw the neatly manicured Purple Prince Crabapple trees that lined each side of the driveway. They looked like soldiers. Their rich-colored flowers burst amidst the luscious green pastures of the sprawling estate. Lydia let down her window to inhale the fragrance of what looked like roses, but she only smelled the fresh country air. Two Bentley Continentals, one black and the other dark red, were parked nose to rear in front of Solara Records. There was a black Range Rover like Sydney's, a couple of Mercedes, and a Lexus 400 parked in the designated parking. The small west side parking lot had a few domestic cars in it and two security officers were posted at the entrance, waiting for Sydney to approach. They spoke to Sydney by her stage name, Tre´, but asked for Lydia's ID. Being that she was an unofficial guest, Lydia was escorted to the main lobby. Lydia watched Sydney until she vanished around the corner of a long corridor. Sydney entered the board room and took a seat at the large round table. She was looking through her bag when Lilo walked in. He walked over and stopped within inches of her. Sydney nervously leered at him as she slightly leaned away from him. She was sure he wasn't crazy enough to handle her with their attorneys in the building but she didn't take her eyes off him. Sydney was convinced Lilo was a real Jekyll and Hyde. Not even two hours ago he was insinuating he wanted to have sex with her and bring her to L.A. for the weekend. Now, he was looking at her with disgust, accusing her of having some serious nerves.

Then he corrected himself, saying she had a pair of nuts for trying to push her frivolous request, "You signed a contract with me," he reminded. Sydney sat quietly as previously instructed by her representative, who knew every detail concerning Lilo and Sydney's interactions. He knew about the relationship, the assaults—verbal, physical, and sexual. Feeling ignored, Lilo intimidated her by suddenly thrusting his hand across the table in her direction. She flinched and gasped. He laughed, thinking he had the upper hand. The attorneys for all sides walked in. Everyone spoke and took their seats. Domino opened the meeting and handed the floor to Solara's attorney, Johnny Godfrey. Johnny "long-winded" Godfrey spoke for nearly an hour, offering his most flowery bulls—t about the contracts, investments, good deeds and expectations. He interpreted all things to Solara's favor as expected, and concluded that Solara had only operated in the artist, Tre´s, best interest.

Francis Iglianno, Sydney's attorney from the WCPA, listened patiently the whole time without saying a single word. Alan Roberts, Lilo's attorney, a Canadian with a dark girl fetish, chimed in next. He recited business codes and the contractual processes—attempting to stone face. He talked about Lilo's reasonable expectations as a manager and his complaints about Sydney being spoiled. Alan boasted that Sydney obviously considered herself as privileged as other, more experienced artists who had been managed by his client, "Artists who'd earned their due," he said.

It took every ounce of Sydney's strength to keep from popping that man on the head with that pitcher of water on the table. Francis waited patiently without interruption or interjection, and after nearly two hours, Francis finally represented Sydney's interest. He spoke assertively about how detrimental a domestic lawsuit would be against a manager who had physically, verbally and sexually abused his subordinate lover. He went on to state that the situation would certainly bleed over into questioning the character and reputation of Solara Records as well. He assured there were individuals who confirmed previous abuses at the hands of Lilo Mims, "Namely, Deja, a former artist who was dropped from the label due to her *non-compliance* to participate in Mr. Lilo Mims', shall we say, unusual tastes…"

Finally, Francis brought to light a clause in Sydney's management contract with the WCPA that prohibited her from entering into any other managerial contract without the express consent of the WCPA, which is a subsidiary of EKG, Inc.

"This is something you as a corporation should have clearly understood, and I assure you the WCPA has not given that consent to anyone. There exists no secondary management of any of the WCPA's primary clients, in any capacity. Furthermore, EKG, Inc. has made a significant investment in Sydney Hebert, which comes with an absolute commitment to protect that investment."

Frank pulled out two documents, one for Mr. Godfrey and one for Mr. Roberts. Whatever they read in those documents, the whole atmosphere changed. Mr. Godfrey and Mr. Roberts talked with their clients and by the end of their private discussions, Domino and Solara Records was pleased with not being included in the possible lawsuit. Lilo's options were few. He could either accept being fired as manager, recouping no further revenue as manager, or face a domestic violence lawsuit, which would include major punitive damages. Ultimately, he would lose his cash cow anyway. Alan recommended Lilo cut his losses and count everything as water under the bridge, instead of fighting. Lilo was intent on making Sydney pay one way or another and attempted to issue a threat, but was quickly warned of the consequences of potentially harming EKG's investment. It was best he remained quiet and move on to the next project. Everything else would be explained to him in another meeting. There were a few times during the meeting when Lilo's caramel face turned red, but that was the first time his face turned as red as it did. He was fuming. If he thought for one second that he could do something without repercussion he would have. But just in case Sydney was wrong about that, she remained seated until Lilo stormed out of the boardroom. Then she arose from the boardroom table feeling ten feet tall—eager to share the news of her freedom, not realizing she wasn't completely free. She rightfully owed Lilo for his production and marketing of her album, which would be paid first, and her percentage coming afterward. Leaving Solara, Sydney excitedly shared everything that happened in the meeting. She called Pamela and repeated everything she'd just told Lydia. She was so excited she trembled. Her voice cracked. She called Julia, who already knew what happened. She encouraged Sydney about how awesome the WCPA is. After hanging up with Julia, Sydney called Marjorie and repeated the same thing, ending that conversation with, "Hell yeah, I'm going to Rich's party. Girl, this is cause for a real celebration," Sydney exclaimed.

Sydney called home to tell David what happened. By then, she was less dramatic, but still giddy. She never actually told him what happened, she just celebrated, calling herself a free agent, and saying she was free to work with other producers. She said Lilo didn't like it, but she admitted that being personally involved with her manager was never a good idea.

Sydney quickly changed the subject and asked David, "So, whatchu doin?" Whatever David said made Sydney frown. She blasted him with a series of questions, "Get a haircut where?... With who?... How did you meet Aaron Seals?... Why did he come to my house?... Yeah, right, and your jealous behind would have a heart attack if I did…I'm not laughing…No…Because I can take you to Michael Anthony's in Atlanta," she finished.

Lydia interjected, "Girl, please let that man go somewhere." Sydney started laughing, "Oh, so now you want me to listen to Lydia…okay…so, she's your friend because she's telling me to let you go?… All right…you can go out and play with your new friend, but you gotta bring your Tasha with you…yes…don't make me muff you when I get home…no, it ain't furry no more," she laughed, "Oh, so you like it furry," she laughed aloud.

"Ugh…both of y'all got issues," Lydia accused.

Sydney back-handed Lydia's thigh, "Hush you." Lydia reached over and pinched Sydney's titty.

"Ouch *heffa*," Sydney squeaked, as she reached over to pinch Lydia's, and she let her.

Sydney continued her scattered conversation with David, answering, "I just pinched Lydia…no…but like I said, take Tasha with you…ok…I'll see y'all when y'all get back silly."
It was a few minutes after five o'clock when Sydney pulled into her garage. Tasha heard them when they came inside and quickly finished entertaining herself. After calming her hormones, and freshening up, Tasha went downstairs but paused to eavesdrop

when she heard Sydney laugh and ask why she had
to be the man.

"Because yours is bigger than mine," Lydia
replied.

Sydney laughed, "No it's not."

"Girl, that thing is a poker compared to mine.

Tasha frowned, saying within, 'What the hell?'

Sydney and Lydia laughed, "Wait, wait,
wait…slow down," Lydia said, "Let me show you
first."

Sydney continued laughing, "Girl, all of this is
new for me."

"I know!" Lydia confirmed, "Which is why you
have to slow down…and feel it."

"Liddy, if we do this any slower, we're gonna be
doing it."

Lydia mumbled something Tasha wasn't able to
make out, but whatever she said, Sydney was
cracking up laughing when she replied, "Yeah, I bet
you would."

At that point, Tasha abruptly walked into the
living area where Sydney and Lydia were and asked,
"What is going on in here?"

"Girl!" Sydney snapped, grabbing her chest.
"You scared me walking in here like that."

"So, what are y'all doing?" Tasha asked,
suspiciously.

Sydney claimed Lydia was teaching her how to Salsa, but Tasha confessed it sounded more like the two of them were about to do the nasty.

"So, what were you coming to do…join in?" Sydney teased.

"Ooh, no shaa…ain't no bumpin cat's gon work over here. This gul gotta have something stiff," Tasha replied.

Sydney ignored Tasha's sarcasm and asked David's whereabouts and why she wasn't with him. Tasha told her that David said he was going to the barbershop and left with some guy in a blue Corvette.

"See, David thinks he's slick…wanna hang with Aaron…ole dog."

CONFLICTED

Ara emotionally sparred with Junior as he stood in the bathroom doorway mean-mugging her—trying to get his way. He wanted her to stay home with him but she couldn't. She had money to make. Private shows and bachelor's parties paid the highest dollar for minimal work, though extra money was on the table for extra services. Furthermore, she and the girls had already agreed to the contract. Junior acted like he was getting that part, and continued staring, waiting for the answer he wanted.

Irritated, Ara snapped, "Lil boy! My answer is not changing. Move around…standing there looking like your daddy," referring to David, the only dad Junior has known.

Junior walked away without saying a word and sat on the couch, still pouting. He sat quietly without mumbling under his breath, which was surprising because that was one of their biggest problems—his smart mouth. How David managed to get Junior to stop being so verbally combative was a mystery, but it was one Ara appreciated because there were plenty of times, she wanted to punch that child in his mouth. Ara walked into the living room already dressed in drag but wearing a thin overcoat. Junior just looked at her with that same flat affect David has when he's annoyed.

"Ugh," Ara frowned, thinking how crazy it was for Junior to act so much like David. Had she not given birth to the little spawn when she did, she would have sworn David was his biological father. "I have to go. I'm gonna get Regina to come over until your grandmother comes to get you. She should be here soon. Give Mama a kiss," Ara requested.

Ara kissed Junior, but he didn't kiss her back. He just looked into her eyes without puckering his lips. They had a brief staring contest—forehead to forehead until Ara conceded. Junior silently looked at her until she closed the door.

Primary entertainment for the bachelor's party was from eight o'clock in the evening to one o'clock in the morning—seven hundred dollars for each dancer. It was four of them. After one o'clock, the fee went up, especially for a group of doctors who were known to spare no expense. The party included all-you-can-drink, but back in the day, Ara learned a hard lesson about mixing alcohol with business. She'd gotten drunk around the wrong clients which resulted in her being gang-raped. She never made that mistake again. The ones who did that to her were thugs, who were only interested in abusing sisters who were just trying to make a living. Ever since that night, Ara looked at all clients as the wrong clients to drink with. The crew of doctors were no different. Things could still go sideways. For the party, the clients requested exotic aliases that were different from their actual stage names. They wanted the names to match the colors they chose for the dancers to wear—Peach Fuzz (Diamond), for the girl in peach, Red Rum (Marquise), for the girl in red, and Juicy Fruit (Chyna), for the girl in yellow.

Ara, aka Fiyah, was Purple Passion. The ladies gave the doctors more than they asked for by way of their colored attire. Their wigs, lipstick, stilettos, fishnets, harlequin masks, nipple covers, thongs, and glitter matched their chosen colors. They even had their own Seagram's Gin bottles that only had about a shot of gin. The rest was water and a few drops of coloring to match. Ten drunk, horny doctors wouldn't know the difference if they drank it themselves. The clients were already primed and ready when the ladies arrived at the Westside Omni Hotel. Eight of the doctors were white—maybe seven. One could pass for Hispanic, but there were two blacks—one dark and the other light-brown. Ara recognized Thaddeus as soon as she walked into the suite. She'd only met him once at Junior's birthday party at Chuck E. Cheese's, but he was easy to remember. He favored Morris Day, except a shade darker and without freckles. Ara was surprised he was there; especially since David had recently mentioned how he thought Thaddeus was good for his mother. David's assumption could have remained true had Thaddeus not already been lit up. His face was already flush and as soon as he laid eyes on Red Rum's breasts, he went at them like he was about to breastfeed. Then he went for Juicy Fruit's butt like it was Charmin Tissue—and she let him squeeze it. Thaddeus grabbed his package—gripped it, hollered when Purple Passion disrobed—completely oblivious to her identity. Liquid courage had him trying to push up on her right then and there. She reminded him that everything comes with a price tag. He immediately pulled out a little stack, and Ara calculated by sight that it was only a few hundred dollars at most.

"I got it!" Thaddeus yelled. "And something tells me you're gonna get all of this money tonight…and I'm gonna get my money's worth from all this…sexincss," Thaddeus flirted, as he rubbed his little stack of money across Purple Passion's breast. He licked his lips, "Mm, mm, mm…"
Ara flirtatiously laughed because showing her money was the same as kissing that money goodbye. She made eye contact with Juicy Fruit, marking Thaddeus as a quick trick. One moment Thaddeus thought he was about to get his freak on with two honeys, but when Juicy Fruit finished him off, *his* party was over. It was ten o'clock.

***

It was ten o'clock when Sydney, David, Lydia, and Tasha arrived at Rich's wooded estate on Carlisle Ln., which was not far from Sydney's place. The twelve thousand square foot spread looked like an oasis in the middle of a forest. Sydney parked and reminded everyone about confidentiality. She said it was unwritten, but it's what everyone expected. Everyone knew the meaning of confidentiality but only Sydney and Lydia knew what to expect at such parties. David expected to see people wilding out, but Tasha was wide-eyed, expecting to catch some eyes. She had that tight black dress screaming at the seams. Approaching the entrance, Sydney whispered to Tasha not to act like a groupie if she saw a celebrity she liked, and reminded her to take it easy on the drinks. She told David not to smile and speak to everyone like he was Mr. Rogers.

"If people want to talk to you, they will," Sydney taught.

"I got-cho Mr. Rogers," David replied.

'You sho do,' Tasha thought.

Lydia moved smoothly and confidently as if nothing Sydney had said applied to her or was new to her. At the entrance there were two clean-shaven brothers wearing suits with bowties. When the crew approached, the brothers greeted the ladies and let all three of them walk inside but they stopped David.

One of them spoke, "Good evening, brother." David paused, wondering what was going on. The brothers claimed it was a simple security precaution and they wanted to make sure no one was carrying any weapons.

"Oh, but you let the women just walk in?" David questioned.

"That's because they'll be checked inside. It's just procedure brother. Hold your arms out like this," he demonstrated.
As the brother frisked David, he asked if he was from the area.

"Nah. I'm from Texas," David replied

"What part?' He asked.

"Beaumont."

"That's near Orange, right?" He questioned.

"Yeah," David answered.

"Yes, I know a brother from Orange. He's a barber. Brother Bryan. You ever go to Orange?" he asked, as he frisked David's left leg, and right leg while he continued looking at David.

David sighed, "I've been there…passing through."
The brother finished frisking David. He thanked him for cooperating and encouraged him to have a good time. Sydney, Tasha, and Lydia were still near the entrance but had already started mingling. Sydney was already engaged in conversation. Three guys were in her face like she was the guest of honor, and she was enjoying every bit of the attention—showing all thirty-twos. She attempted a couple of times to introduce her little crew but with the

constant interruptions, she couldn't. When David approached her, she encouraged him to have fun but not to disappear. Mingling was easy for a pretty face and a nice thick and chunky in a black pencil dress. Tasha got scooped up quickly and given a personal escort to the bar. David stood next to Lydia and complimented her on how nicely she wore her black dress and heels. She walked away, leaving him to eat her dust. He played it off but quickly found redemption smiling at him by the fireplace. Marjorie was standing there in a white swing dress and white heels with a single ankle strap—looking rather delicious. Despite having someone in her face, she motioned for David to come to her. Feeling chosen, he walked towards her in all his cockiness. Her company walked away, leaving David to feel like he was the replacement.

He flirted, "Girl, look at you…looking like a popsicle on a hot day."
Marjorie laughed and asked where did he think he was going with that corny line.

"Corny? Girl that line earned me the pimp of the year award," David joked.

Marjorie laughed aloud, partially covering her nose and mouth, "Okay pimp Daddy…you might wanna revise that line though."

"Hush before I kiss you right in the mouth," David teased.

"And if you do, I'm gonna kiss your ass right back," Marjorie threatened.

David playfully moved closer, and Marjorie moved her glass to the side and challenged him, "Try me. I ain't playin," she promised.
David leaned towards Marjorie's lips but cowardly backed up—laughing.

"Mm-hmm…just what I thought. Sydney got you trained real good," she dragged.

David smacked, "Girl, pleasc."

"It's all good cat daddy. You're safe with me. Just don't start nothin and it won't be nothin," she warned.

"Well, I ain't trying to start nothin, but you got this lil corner over here smelling pretty darn good—stimulating my senses. What's that fragrance?" David inquired.

"Me," Marjorie answered.

"You?"

"Yes, me," Majorie assured.

"So, you smell like that all over?" David wondered.

"You wanna find out?" she asked.

David laughed, "Girl…you like talking trash huh?"

"And can back every bit of it up too," she assured.

"Yeah…you just better be glad you are off limits," David claimed.

"Off limits? What do you mean?" Marjorie wondered.

"Shid…Syd made it a point that all of her friends are off limits to me," David explained.

"Oh really?" Marjorie wandered. "That's odd because none of my friends are off limits to her," Marjorie corrected. She pointed at Sydney, spryly holding Rich's attention. "Rich is actually a friend of mine. I introduced her to him a while back."

"Yeah, but that's just business," David assumed.

Marjorie let his assumption stand, but she encouraged him not to misunderstand her. She claimed to understand why Sydney may have told him to stay away from her friends but she questioned, "What if one of those friends is feeling you? What do you do with that?"

"You and me? Psst…I don't make enough money for you," David claimed.

Insulted, Marjorie checked him, "Whoa…wait a minute. Are you calling me a gold-digger?"

"Didn't you date two professional football players?" David questioned.

"And a pro basketball player," Marjorie added. "But that doesn't make me a gold digger. That just says I think I'm worth more than a happy meal…and there's nothing wrong with that," she defended.

"It's all good lil mama," David claimed.

"No, it's not. You obviously got some bad information about me. I'm not a gold digger…I'm really not," Marjorie explained, "Yes, I like money. My dad has money. I grew up with nice things. I like nice things. I buy nice things. I think all women like nice things, but at the end of the day, what *I* really want is a good man."

David looked surprised. Marjorie piqued his interest, "Seriously," she continued, "I think most women want a good man…especially if he has potential and is actually *using* that potential. Most of us would be happy to do whatever we have to do to help him get where he's trying to get. We'll spend our last on him. I know I will," Marjorie assured.

David licked his lips and playfully encouraged Marjorie to keep talking dirty to him. She laughed, but that cute laugh turned into an immediate frown, of disgust, "What is he doing here?" Marjorie balked.

David looked to see who Marjorie was talking about and was shocked when he saw the huge brute, "That's who you're dating? Dexter Houston? The Falcon's defensive end?" David questioned.

"Was!" Marjorie corrected, before sliding directly in front of David to hide between his broad shoulders.

"Dang lil mama…that dude is huge," David acknowledged.

"Duh," she replied, as she peeped around David to see where Dexter was headed. She saw him standing, looking around like he was looking for someone. He dapped someone who directed his attention to where Marjorie and David were standing. As soon as Marjorie's location was compromised, she put on a little show, acting like she was totally into David. She launched into a fake conversation and laughed like David had said the funniest thing she'd heard.

She touched David's chest, rubbed his arm, and whispered for him to act like he was her date, "No, my new man…no, my date…yea, just be my date," she decided.

"Marjorie, I ain't getting in no fight over you. I will leave you standing right here," David promised. Marjorie laughed aloud again and posed as though she was mesmerized by what David was saying—despite him acting silly. Marjorie flipped her hair and sipped her drink without breaking eye contact with David. She put her glass up to David's lips for him to sip, confident Dexter had seen all of it.

"Uh oh…he's coming," Marjorie whispered without moving her lips.

David acted like he was about to walk off, but Marjorie grabbed him to make him stay put. She promised Dexter wasn't going to do anything, that he was just a big teddy bear. But from where David was standing, there was nothing teddy about that bear. Dexter was six feet six inches and weighed two hundred seventy-five pounds according to his profile. Marjorie's assurance led David to expect him to be a gentleman when he approached. As David had done when he first approached Marjorie at the fireplace, Dexter did the same. He approached Marjorie as though David was invisible, and asked for her attention. Marjorie directed Dexter's attention to David to make him acknowledge him, but Dexter ignored her intentions.

She forced an introduction, "Dexter…this is David. David this is my *ex*-boyfriend, Dexter," Marjorie said, emphasizing, ex.

David spoke but Dexter mean-mugged him for a few seconds before saying, "What's up little man?" David shook his head and resigned to walk away peacefully, but then Dexter popped off for no reason, challenging David with the universal sign of saying what's up. Dexter's outstretched arms looked like tree trunks. David looked at Dexter, thinking he only had two options if Dexter came at him—a right foot to Dexter's nuts, followed by the hardest left cross to the temple he ever delivered. The second option was the same as the first, but running like hell afterwards. A third option unexpectedly popped up. Marjorie activated that Parliament-Funkadelic control. She told him to come with her and Dexter followed her like a big, over-grown puppy. As soon as David's heart stopped pounding, he went to find Sydney. She and Rich were standing by the pool. As David approached, he heard Rich say something to Sydney about her *long tail,* right before Sydney looked back. As was his comfort level, David walked up and bear-hugged Sydney from behind, mashing his face against hers. He made a long kissing sound, and Rich fired the first shot, "So, this must be your brother?"

David was still holding Sydney when he fired back, "Yep…I'm big brother this week. Next week I'll be her cousin, and the week after that, her homeboy. Then she'll be saying, *Oh, he's just my friend,*" David teased.

Sydney laughed, calling David silly, but she liked every bit of it. She formally introduced them, "Rich…this is my best friend David…who is like brother," she assured, "David, meet Rich."
Rich responded cordially, but David got silly—going overboard with the word, rich.

"David, that's enough! Now, go play," Sydney pushed.

"Nah, all jokes aside man, you really have a nice place. I appreciate the invite," David replied.
Rich gave David a salute, a subtle gesture—telling him to beat it. Sydney looked at Rich as if to tell him to stop it too. As soon as David walked away, Rich continued his conversation, which led to an invite to follow him upstairs. He led, Sydney followed, and Lydia intercepted, asking Sydney where she thought she was going.

"I think we're going to his studio," Sydney answered, attempting to continue.

Lydia grabbed Sydney's arm—tightening her grip, "Sydney."

"What Liddy?"

"You think you are going to his studio?" Lydia questioned.

"Well, that's where we're going," Sydney answered, giggling.

"Sydney, I don't see what's funny."
Sydney tightened her lips to hide the smirk. She asked Lydia if she was being jealous again, and Lydia denied she was, but that she was trying to figure out why she'd taken vacation.

"To spend time with me," Sydney answered.

"But you're spending your time with everyone else," Lydia accused.

"Liddy, play fair and just give me a moment…please. I'm just seeing what he has to offer. Okay? That's all. I promise," Sydney assured. She teasingly pinched Lydia's cheeks as if she were a child and told her to keep an eye on David for her.

"I'm sure perv is just fine, but it seems someone needs to keep an eye on you," Lydia remarked. Sydney winked at Lydia and joined Rich at the bottom of the stairs. Rich unlatched the red rope and assisted Sydney by the hand. Before Rich went up behind Sydney, he told one of the gatekeepers to keep an eye out for the guy with the Orange and White Izod shirt and matching sneakers—referring to David, "He's not allowed upstairs at all." Rich called his studio a sanctuary. It was set up for a live session. Without hesitation or permission, Sydney mounted the piano, and played what appeared to be a spontaneous melody. The verses she sang were from a song Rich had written for the three-time Grammy Award-winning group, Around the Way, entitled "Breathe." Sydney's spontaneity on the piano impressed Rich.

His compliments were almost excessive, "You are a gifted athlete, but music handpicked you."

Sydney believed Rich's words and they motivated her to continue playing melody after melody until time had slipped away. Before she knew it, an hour had passed. Meanwhile, David returned to the pool area looking for Sydney. She wasn't there but Tasha suddenly appeared behind him, wrapping her arms around him from behind. She was toasted, boldly expressing her thoughts, suggesting the two of them disappear for a moment.

She moved in front of him and reminded him of what she'd seen of him already, "Tall…handsome…wet skin…with a towel wrapped around your waist, and that nice…bulge. Man, I was ready to sit you down in that chair and…," Tasha wiped the corners of her mouth, insinuating, exactly what she would have done.

"Girl, how much have you had to drink?" David asked, concerned, and also agitated by her antics. Tasha counted one finger at a time until she held up four fingers, but admitted she had five rounds.

"Feeling pretty good huh?"

"Yep, but I bet you can make me feel better. C'mon, swing out with me," she suggested, rocking her hips to the song, Rock Steady, by the whispers. David began to swing out with Tasha, mildly, just enough to stay on beat. She sang the words as she slowly started improvising her moves—mixing in a little zydeco grind here and there. When Tasha went a little too far, attempting to openly grind on him, instead of pushing her away, he squeezed her, and whispered for her to stop. Tasha continued and David squeezed tighter and told her to stop again, except that time he stopped dancing.

Tasha went in for the kill, "Okay, it's time for us to do this. Let's go," she said, attempting to drag David after her.

He pulled her back and she exaggerated her crashing back into him—laughing. She locked her arms around his waist and let her head fall completely back, looking up at him. She told him to stop acting like he was scared of her and gave him another, not-so-subtle grind, "You need to get this," she said.

"Hey…" David cautioned.

Tasha laughed and responded with an aggressive thrust. David shook Tasha, and firmly told her through gritted teeth, "Stop this bulls—t." Deeply offended, Tasha snatched herself from David's grasp and walked away, making everything bounce—hair, breast and hips—advertising. The very thing David tried to avoid, happened. Tasha's hurt feelings caused a disturbing scene.

A brother nearby, warned David not to let his woman get away, "That's a fine woman, brother."

"No doubt," David replied. *Just not the one I'm looking for,* he thought.

David hesitated to go after Tasha, thinking it would add to an already questionable circumstance. He walked out onto the terrace instead, and saw Lydia standing a short distance away. She was near Thuja trees, gazing. She looked like she had lost her best friend, but when she saw David approaching, he heard her sigh from a distance. David walked right into Lydia's personal space like he belonged there, and acted like he was trying to see what she was looking at.

Lydia didn't move. She only shook her head, annoyed, "Man…why are you always messing with me? I wasn't bothering you. I was just out here minding my own business, thinking my own thoughts, and enjoying this scenery…and here you come."

"You all right?" David asked.

Lydia sighed, "I'm *fine.*"

"You sho right about that," David replied, as he leaned back to look at Lydia's butt.

Lydia closed her eyes and exhaled. She shook her head again, wondering why David had to be so aggravating. David waited for Lydia to snap on him, roll her eyes at him, or tell him to go screw himself, or something close to that, but she didn't. In a calm voice, she asked if he was looking for Sydney, hoping he was, so that he could leave her alone.

He licked his lips, "Actually…I was looking for you…witcho lil sexy self."

Lydia chuckled, thinking, *this dude here.* Again, she asked David in the calmest voice possible, "Why…do you insist on messing with me?"

"Because I like you," David replied

Lydia tightened her lips as if she was trying especially hard not to give David what he was asking for—a good cussing out. Somehow, in some way, she managed to hold back. She decided to play his little game for as long as she could. Lydia took a sip of her champagne, turned to face David, as if she was interested in his presence, and asked him what he liked about her. She expected him to say something completely off the wall, or something sexual, but without hesitation, David admitted that he liked her attitude.

Shocked by what he said, Lydia asked for clarification, "My attitude?"

"Yes, your attitude," David confirmed. His tone and facial expression were serious when he concluded, "I love the way you speak your mind. I don't think anyone has to wonder how you feel about them, or what you're thinking. I like that about you."

David continued, mentioning a few other things he liked about her, such as her confidence, her love for sports, and her sense of style. He thought she was cool—in a sexy, tomboyish kind of way. He admitted to feeling that way the first time they met and actually believed they were cool when she and Syd stayed at his place, mainly because of how they all chilled together, "We cooked, laughed, and stuff. What did I do to make you so salty with me?" Lydia cleared her throat before asking David if he really wanted to know the answer to that question. He did. So, Lydia positioned herself as if she was about to run down a whole laundry list of things that he'd done that irked her nerves, but then she admitted he really hadn't done anything to her. It was what he had done to Sydney that weekend they stayed. She recalled waking up and seeing him and Sydney doing the do in the same room,

"Everything was just right there, and I felt violated."

David laughed, defending his actions, claiming Sydney was the one who initiated that.

"Wrong!" Lydia corrected, "I saw what you were doing to her in the bed first, and after she got her jollies off, that's when she got out of the bed and joined you on the futon…which was worse, because like I said, everything was just there," she explained, with her hands.

"So, why does that make me the bad guy?" David questioned. "I would have done the same with you…"

"What?" Lydia snapped

"I'm just saying if you and I were like me and Syd are," he explained.

"Ok then, correct that, because me and you would never happen," Lydia replied, rolling her eyes.

"Well, that's too bad," David said, revealing that if he had met her under different circumstances, he would have been interested. "I would have approached you."

David's words created an awkward moment for Lydia. She thought the champagne must have produced an extra kick, because she couldn't believe she was feeling what she thought she was feeling, especially not with David. She casually put some extra space between them, but David closed the gap. That's when Lydia realized she was feeling his energy—positive energy. It caught her off guard, and surprised her. She knew she should have at least acknowledged his professed attraction, but she couldn't. She didn't want to provoke him to say something that would mess up the moment. So, to keep from provoking him to say something that would ruin the momentary good space, she opted for a bathroom break. It was her way of escape, but when she asked him if he wanted to come, as soon as those words fell from her lips, she knew David would latch onto them like a Pitbull, and he did.

"You mean like us…coming together?" he asked.

"Ha! You wish," Lydia answered.

David faked gasped, "Get your mind out of the gutter, Liddy. I'm only talking about escorting you to the bathroom," he claimed.

"Yeah, right. I know how your little perverted mind works—just like somebody else I know," Lydia assured.

"Seriously," David claimed. "But then again… since you think that's what I was thinking… maybe we can, uh…" David playfully suggested.

"Boy, please," Lydia snapped. "You better go find somebody you can handle."
David burst into laughter at Lydia's comeback, and Lydia had to laugh at herself for even going there with David. It just came out, and it was funny. She actually gave David a soft high-five when he put his hand up for one. Still, she quickly reminded him that they were not friends and that he still gets on her nerves. She walked off, claiming the bathroom was still calling her name. David watched as she walked away, admiring, and almost as if Lydia had eyes in

the back of her head, she quickly turned and told David to stop looking at her butt. Then she proceeded to walk with her hands clasped behind her back, hiding her butt from David's gaze. Before she made it inside, thinking David was still looking, and he was, playfully stuck out her tongue at him, imitating Sydney.

HELLO STRANGER

Fifteen minutes had passed and Lydia hadn't returned from the bathroom. She didn't say she was coming back but David assumed she would since they'd hit a good spot. After waiting another five minutes, David decided on an attempt to go upstairs.

One of the gatekeepers asked to see David's stamp, "No stamp, no entry," he said. Concerned, David said he only wanted to make sure his friend was alright because she'd been up there for a while. Both gatekeepers laughed and gave each other dap.

One assured David, "If she's been up there for a while, then she's doing just fine. Trust me."

David risk making himself look stupid by asking if there was a private party going on upstairs. The gatekeepers ignored his question, but when two females walked up, David was told to step aside. He watched them go up without having to show a stamp, and got the message. Immediately, wild images formed in his mind about what Sydney might be doing upstairs. Images of he doing, and getting done. They came in like a flurry—too many to suppress, so he just wondered if she'd gone upstairs too. He questioned himself, why he was looking for any of them anyway, they weren't his responsibility. Everyone was grown. He found himself near the bar, wondering if he should order a drink. As he contemplated, a beautiful stranger with box braids, dressed in a stone-washed jacket and jeans came alongside him. Her arm brushed against his, but she didn't say excuse me, and David didn't move. She ordered a rum and Coke and a Cognac on the rocks.

David assumed she was getting drinks for herself and someone else, but she handed him the Cognac, "You look like a Hennessey man…especially by your taste in women."

David smiled as he took the cup and sipped, "And what is my taste in women?"

"Thick and pretty…wearing a black dress. That's your girl, right?" she responded.

David assumed the stranger was referring to Tasha by the description, thick, but denied she was his girl.

"You sure about that? You had her wrapped up by the pool earlier," she confirmed.

David took another small sip before assuring the stranger that the thick and pretty girl in the black dress, that he was actually trying to calm down by the pool, was not his girl.

The stranger saw Tasha approaching from David's rear, and gave him a grin, "Okay."

After detecting a flirtatious interaction between David and a female, Tasha sought to stop whatever was starting to brew between the two. She walked up and stepped right in between him and little Ms. Cutie, bringing her heavy hips to a hard stop, with one hand on her hip and her head cocked to the left, all in one smooth motion. She looked at David as if to ask him what he thought he was doing. David smiled and attempted to gently side-sweep her so he could proceed with his conversation. At first, she didn't move, despite David nudging her. When she realized he seriously wanted her to move, she moved. Feeling dissed, Tasha rolled her eyes at him and walked off as she did earlier—advertising.

Little Ms. Cutie gloated, "Gone in less than a minute."

She blew her nails and stroked them across her stone-wash jacket as if to polish them. She held up her glass for a toast, and introduced herself, as Fin-D. David toasted, and introduced himself as D, before pointing towards a cozy spot for them. Fin-D acknowledged seeing David come in as part of Sydney's group. She figured he had to be crushing something terrible on one of them, because why else would girls bring a dude with them to a party, she questioned. David chuckled, neither confirming nor denying, Fin-D's assumption. Instead, he admitted to his lifelong friendship with Sydney.

"Me and that girl go way back to baby bottles and pacifiers," he said.

"So, y'all like family?" Fin-D investigated. David confirmed and attempted to move the conversation towards Fin-D, asking about her name, and wondering if it was Fendi, like the bag.

She said her name slower, pronouncing the syllables, "Fin...D, but my name is Finetta." David took a chance at adding some humor, asking if *Fin* was short for Fine, and whether the *D* was short for Damn, as in Damn you fine.

Fin-D dropped her head and laughed a little before asking, "You know that's corny right?" David nodded, knowing it was, but he also knew it worked because she was smiling.

Fin-D asked him what was D short for, and David mumbled, "Ain't nothing short here."

Fin-D burst out laughing, "Okay…okay, I guess I stepped right into that one," she admitted.

"Yes, you did" David answered, "And if this was a boxing match you would be looking at the ceiling right about now."

"Knocked smooth out huh?" Fin-D replied, still chuckling.

David told her his name and thirty minutes later they were still talking and picking each other's brains. They soon moved to a quieter spot and eventually, Fin-D led David into the quiet lounge beyond a set of French doors at the end of one of the hallways. That's when she revealed some of her talents. Fin-D was a singer and one-third of a girl group called TIF—a moniker for Toni, Izzy, and Finetta. They had recently signed to Rich's label and though some songs were complete, their lead single hadn't been chosen and released. She was a little frustrated by that because she was still living with her mom in Carver Homes in southeast Atlanta.

"It's just hard being around so much money and none of it is mine. I'm ready for a life change," she admitted.

"Girl, you're speaking my love language," David replied.

Fin-D found David's admission interesting. She'd never heard a masculine dude use such an emotional expression. She asked him to explain what he meant by that. David explained, that as an undefeated boxer, he really hadn't made any real money. Like her, he was in association with someone with money, but he wanted his own too.

"But you said, love language. Why did you use that expression?" she asked directly.

David didn't really know how to explain why he used that terminology. It just came out. He said it felt like she connected with him when she said what she said.

"To be honest, that connection felt like…I don't know…hell…like we kissed or something," he laughed.

Fin-D nodded in the affirmative, "I get it…I get it. I like it."

Despite only knowing each other for less than an hour, the two hit a comfort level with each other where laughter, touches and strong eye contact adorned their interaction. David mused over them seeing each other again. They had to hang out while he was there, as well as keep in touch after he went back to Texas. Fin-D agreed. She liked the idea, and actually wished the night could last a bit longer, but her regular life and her regular job that she had to go to later on that morning, demanded the night come to an end. Cinderella had to get home. Before leaving, Fin-D decided to go to the bathroom first, which was through the doorway of the lounge area where they were sitting, and a short distance down the hallway. David agreed to wait in the lounge for her. Fin-D went, but returned quickly, looking as if she'd seen something traumatizing.

Timidly, she asked David, "Are you sure that thick, pretty girl is not your girl?"

"Nah," David confirmed, adding that she is Sydney's younger cousin. "Why?"

"Because… if she is your girl, your girl is getting knocked down in that bathroom."

David sprang to his feet, "She's getting jumped?"

Fin-D stopped him, "No! She's not getting jumped. She's in the bathroom getting busy," she explained.

David settled himself and Tasha walked into the lounge area, freshening her dress and looking slightly disheveled, wanting to explain. All David wanted to know was if she was fine, and if it was consensual, and the fact Tasha was there trying to explain what was going on, made it obvious. She was doing what she wanted to do.

Meanwhile, Lydia was feeling a bit isolated and ready to go. Sydney was still upstairs, doing God knows what, and Tasha had been missing in action for about as long as Sydney. David had simply ghosted her, and though she casually looked around for him for nearly an hour, thinking he would be easy to spot in his orange and white shirt, he was nowhere to be found. Lydia decided to go upstairs, but just as she was about to, the color orange in her peripheral vision caught her attention. She looked. It was David, who'd just come through the French doors at the end of the hallway. As soon as he vanished, Tasha followed, exiting through the same doors. Immediately, Lydia pursued them, passing through the crowd, cussing in her mind, convinced they'd been up to no good. Reaching the French doors, she saw the outside door and rushed after them, but they were gone. She went left towards the rear of the home before turning around and going towards the front. Finding no trace of them, Lydia went to investigate what was beyond the French doors. It was empty and dimly lit. She figured David and Tasha had gone as low as they possibly could, and considering the brevity of Tasha's dress, it would have been easy to do. Lydia knew then that she had to go upstairs to tell Sydney what she had just witnessed.

Now, Marjorie had just returned to Rich's party, parking a short distance from the house. Before getting out, she opened a miniature bottle of vodka and was downing it as David and a girl passed by. Marjorie nearly choked, but David was so engrossed in his conversation with the box-braided cutie that he didn't see her in the car. Marjorie watched them standing next to the silver Suzuki Samurai, laughing and touching like new lovers. They hugged, and even after the cutie got into her Jeep, they continued talking for another ten minutes. Marjorie expected a kiss, but the cutie only got out for another hug before driving away.

On his way back towards Rich's, Marjorie let David pass her car a little before she got out, "Hey, where you going, hot boy?" she asked.

David recognized Marjorie's voice and did a quick about-face, "Hey, what up, sexy?" He approached her and hugged her, and although she returned the gesture, she warned him about hugging her so much. He responded, teasing her with a threat to kiss her as he had teased earlier.

As she had done earlier, she dared him to do it, "I will get in your throat," she threatened.

"And if you do, we'll be rolling around in the grass," David replied.

"Then we'll just be rolling around in the grass," Marjorie promised, before asking Sydney's whereabouts.

David smacked, "Man, that knucklehead is still upstairs."

"Dang… you alright?" she asked, feeling his disappointment with Sydney.

David nodded his head, claiming he was cool, but Marjorie could tell he wasn't. He almost looked disgusted. She invited him to sit in the car so she could pick his brain. They talked for about thirty-minutes—picking up where they left off before being interrupted by Dexter. Marjorie wasn't a gold-digger after all. She just called her own shots, and she learned that David didn't tell his business, or slander his girl—something Marjorie found valuable in a man. With that conclusion, they decided it was best if he showed his face again at the party.

Between his conversation in the car with her, and the time he spent with, whom Marjorie referred to as little Ms. Cutie, David had been gone for a while. On the way back, Marjorie stopped to talk with someone she knew. David kept going. Before he reached the entrance to the party, Sydney stormed out of Rich's mansion in a rage. She saw David, and without a heartbeat's pause, lunged at his chest, screaming 'dirty bastard!' In one motion, upon impact, David grabbed her arms and slung her around, her feet left the ground. His emotions went from zero to one-hundred, asking her what was going on. She screamed for him to let her go, as she continued firing insults— "You sorry, no-good bastard!" She jerked and flailed to get away from him, causing a dramatic scene. She tried to stomp his foot with the heel of her shoe and kick his shin, but when she missed both attempts, she spit in his face. David pushed and jerked, and yelled, asking what was wrong with her. He looked at Lydia with desperation in his eyes, looking for answers, and Sydney spit in his face a second time. David let one of her arms go so he could wipe his face and Sydney started hitting with her free hand. David blocked the licks with his free hand and lunged, shoving her backwards with his forearm. Sydney threw her truck keys towards his face. He ducked. Lydia thought David was about to go at Sydney and she grabbed around his neck from behind. Somehow, whatever David did, he and Lydia wound up face to face and before he knew it, he had jacked her up by her underarms. He was about to slam her, but when he saw security was rushing towards him, barking commands, he tossed her away from him. David started back pedaling to keep some distance between him and security. He snatched off his shirt, ready to deal with whatever was about to go down. He was locked in on security, but he could see Sydney running in the direction of where she parked with Lydia and Tasha following. He saw

Marjorie's white dress heading in the same direction. A few seconds later, as he was partially surrounded, he heard the sound of Sydney's truck speeding away.

Then a voice yelled, "AT EASE SOLDIERS! At ease!"

A brown-skinned brother about David's height and build came into view, giving the same command to David, "At ease, brother."

The guy approached David with his palms up but David warned him not to walk up on him, "I'm telling you, bruh. If you walk up on me, it's gon be some sh—t!"

The guy assured David that he didn't want any trouble, but he promised David that if he didn't back down, it wasn't going to turn out too good for him, "These brothers are not going to let you make it out of here. Tell me what's going on, so we can work this out," he said.

David never dropped his stance. His adrenaline was pumping. He knew he was disadvantaged, but he'd already decided that he was not going to be the only one going down. Somebody was going to be filled with regret. The guy continued standing with his palms up, requesting David's attention, asking again what was going on. David cussed, saying he didn't know what was going on. He just didn't want another person running up to him.

The guy promised him no one was going to run up on him if he calmed down, "But if you don't calm down, we have to keep everyone here safe. Understand? Now, what can I do to help you, brother?" he asked.

David had to think about that question because apart from not wanting anyone to run up on him, he didn't know how anyone could help him. Everything was chaotic, and he was alone. The guy picked up David's shirt from off the lawn and tossed it to him. He introduced himself as Qadir. He said he was a minister and that he owned the security company that was providing security for the owner of the property.

David introduced himself, and referred to himself as a childhood friend of Sydney Hebert, "Which is crazy, because we've always been so close. I have no clue what all this was about. None!" David expressed.

Qadir agreed. Everything was crazy, but he informed David of the responsibility he had to the owner of the property. He had to escort David off the property and make sure he remained a certain distance away from the property. That meant David would have to walk away or call a cab. Marjorie came back to check on David while he and Qadir were standing at the curbside. She appeared to give him the cold shoulder and wouldn't give him a ride, especially not to Sydney's house, and especially without knowing what was going on. After thirty minutes of waiting for a taxi, David and Qadir got an understanding of each other. They both loved boxing. One of the members of his security team was a boxer and was also the cousin of Erol Bryson. When David claimed he could beat Bryson, that opened up a moment of harmless trash talk—simple bonding. The taxi arrived, prepared to bring David to Sydney's place, but Qadir made a last-minute suggestion. He urged David to get a room for the night, informing him that a domestic issue was not something he wanted to deal with in Georgia. He suggested the Clarion Hotel which was less than twenty minutes away. His sister worked there. He couldn't promise David a discount, but he guaranteed it would be a nice place to cool off. The taxi brought David to the Clarion and Marjorie pulled in right behind the taxi. She called him to the car and told him to get in. Her brother was out of town for the weekend and she had a key to his condo. That's where she wanted to bring him. It was her hangout when she didn't want to be found. David was cool with that because he really didn't want to be alone. When they arrived at Marjorie's brother's condo, she invited him to make himself comfortable. David admired the décor. It was eccentric—a nice selection of African art, weird sculptures, and abstract paintings. The furniture was contemporary with angles—asymmetric, but very inviting. There was one ashtray on the coffee table and coasters on every end table. The smell of fresh, dampness filled the air. It was thick, almost as if David could taste it. It was soothing to his senses. It reminded him of the times he smelled rain in the air.

"Man, it smells good in here. What is that?" David asked, inhaling deeply.

"I'm not sure, but my brother is into fragrances. He actually has a perfume coming out soon. As a matter of fact, I'm wearing one of his fragrances," she replied with a smile.

"I thought you told me that was you," David said, giving Marjorie the side eye.

"Actually, when you asked me what I was wearing, I told you it was Me.

"So, it ain't you."

"Me is the name of the fragrances, silly. Now, do you still want to know if the rest of me smells like Me?" Marjorie teased.

David shot back, "Keep playing and I will have you smelling like me."

"Please do," Marjorie replied with mischief in her eyes.

David and Marjorie's constant flirting and testing each other's game temperature, from day one, had finally brought them to a moment of show and tell. They were both game. It could have gone down right then and there, but since it had been a long day for both of them, freshening up a bit was a good idea. While visibly excited, David was ready to take full advantage of the moment, except for the roadblock. He didn't have any condoms with him. He didn't plan for anything and certainly not that moment.

Marjorie admired his caution, and assured him she had him covered, "In the meantime, you can find something strong at the bar…help yourself," she encouraged.

Marjorie grabbed her purse and went to freshen up. Before getting into the scalding hot shower, she popped a black mollie and chased it with another miniature bottle of vodka. When she finished showering, she wrapped herself in a towel and opened the door to a half-naked David, wearing only his boxers. His jeans and shirt were neatly folded and placed at the foot of the bed. Majorie quickly sexed him over with her eyes from head to toe before suggesting he make his shower quick. When David finished his shower, he entered the room, and heard a message he really didn't want to hear.

Marjorie's brother was actually out of condoms. When she said it, she saw the let down on David's face briefly, but he quickly recovered, and she was glad he did. Maybe it was David's anger towards Sydney that provoked a desire of recklessness, or perhaps it was Marjorie's, pretty girl malice, but the sexual chemistry between them demanded a fight night. The cat and mouse game they'd been playing had come to the end of the road, and David was convinced Marjorie could do every bit of what she looked like she could do. He slid under the sheet, and like a well-choreographed dance, Marjorie rolled to her side, her back to him, allowing David's body to mold against hers. Feeling his immediate readiness, Marjorie positioned her hips, granting David an unobstructed pathway to the beginning of a slow, savoring dance. Like him, and to his welcoming surprise, Marjorie was a grinder. With one hand, she pressed against the bed, using it as leverage to press her hips back against him, ensuring a deeper connection. Her nails dug into David's thigh as he penetrated her to his fullest extent—she exhaled, almost as if she was being relieved of a nagging pain. From the beginning to the end of that first round, their bodies communicated, rhythmically. Every dance throughout the remainder of the dark morning, Marjorie kept her back towards

David, allowing him to work out his frustration and pain—healing the wounds Sydney had inflicted on him. She avoided face-to-face in an attempt to keep from becoming too entangled. The mix between David's addictive properties and her recreational relaxants were mixing a little too well—a perfect rush of pleasure. It would build, swell and burst and spill. It would do it again and with a complete exhale, she would drift and not even realize they'd fallen asleep. During their moments of rest and napping between their dance sessions, Marjorie was careful not to rest in David's arms, with her face against his chest, listening to his heartbeat. He was giving off that kind of energy that can make a woman exhale in surrender. Marjorie refused to do that with him. He wasn't hers. However, when he woke up that last time, he tried to do something as if she was his, that thing that scares most independent women—he attempted missionary. Marjorie stopped him, because she wasn't his. She warned him that if he did it like that, he would have to kiss her while he was doing it. David was cool with that and attempted to proceed, but Marjorie stopped him.

She pushed against David's shoulders, lifting him, and warned him again, making it clear, "If you kiss me while doing it like this, then you're my man," she insisted.

"But you got a man," David remarked.

"Then I'll have two…and I'm very possessive," she hissed.

"Then what do you want me to do?" David questioned.

"Either turn me over and get it, or do it like this and get me. The choice is yours," she threatened with sort of a smile.

The few seconds of looking into each other's eyes seemed like minutes. Marjorie looked as if she was telling David to go for it, but again, she looked like as if she were warning him to make the right decision. Passion urged him to go through with it, but boxer instinct warned against it. He flipped her onto her stomach, and again, during their final dance later, in the shower, Marjorie nearly buckled. If the neighbors hadn't heard anything before that moment, they did then. It was the summit of Marjorie's pleasure. It was also afternoon, and David was starving. He hadn't eaten since Friday night before going to Rich's party. While Marjorie admitted to not exactly being domesticated, she did order delivery for them. They ate and finally talked about the confrontation that happened at Rich's.

David told Marjorie what he knew, which was nothing. Apart from the confrontation, he was clueless, "Sydney never said why she was mad. She just kept calling me out of my name and trying to fight."

Marjorie wondered, "Do you think it was because of that lil cutie you were with?"
David shook his head, denying Fin-D could've been the problem. He'd only walked her to her car, and before that, they were inside Rich's place, chilling and talking like everyone else.

"We just hit a cool spot and gelled, you know? But even if it was something more, Sydney didn't have to come at me like that. She put me in a bad spot."
Marjorie agreed, the whole scene was ugly, but what surprised her most was how Sydney left him as she did, "She virtually put you in my hands."

David wondered, "Did you plan this?"

"More like seized the opportunity. "Especially when you asked me if I could give you a ride."

"But you ignored me."

"Of course, I did. That was in case she came back looking for you. I didn't want anybody saying you left with me."

David nodded, "Makes sense."
He glanced at the clock on the wall—two o'clock. A heavy sigh escaped, as he rubbed his hands over his waves several times, alternating the left and right. Preparing to leave started to feel like regret. It wasn't

because he wanted to stay with Marjorie, though he was welcomed. She had the condo until Sunday evening, but it was more about not wanting to see Sydney. The lingering effects of what she did, and the dangerous predicament she put him in was unforgiveable. David resolved, the best thing for him to do was to go home.

Marjorie understood his reasoning for wanting to go home, but she couldn't help feeling a bit slighted by his decision. "I really wish you wouldn't leave so abruptly, considering…" she confessed, leering. Then she chuckled and suggested before she just let him fly back to Texas after getting her stuff, she would have to stash him away in a hotel for at least a couple of days, "Nah…just kidding…sort of. Honestly though, whatever you decide, I know you have to go to Sydney's first, and I think it's worth knowing before you get there, what's going on with her. I would hate for you to walk into something blind," she said.

Marjorie suggested she call Sydney and put her on speaker. The thought of hearing Sydney's voice only agitated him more, but he agreed. Marjorie called. Sydney answered, and David listened, quietly. Sydney was frantic. She'd been crying and hadn't slept. She was hurt, and pissed because David had left the party with some female. Marjorie asked who David left with and Sydney described the girl as a little brown-skinned female with braids.

Marjorie corrected her, "He didn't leave with that girl. I saw them. He walked her to her car. They talked for a bit, but he didn't leave with her. I was parked across the street from them."

"But he was gone for over an hour!" Sydney barked.

"Baby, after that girl left, David was heading back to the party, and I stopped him and asked where you were. He said you were still upstairs. We sat in the car and talked for about thirty-minutes."

"Marjorie, please tell me you're lying," Sydney begged.

"No, I'm not. We talked for at least thirty-minutes…and that was after that girl drove off," Marjorie assured.
Sydney became overly dramatic, saying, "Please tell me I didn't lose my sh—t on David for nothing."

Marjorie answered, "I think you did, because he was talking to me for most of that time."
Marjorie took Sydney off speaker and motioned for David to give her a moment. She got off the sofa and walked to the bedroom to finish her conversation in private. She was in the room for about two or three minutes before returning, looking a bit disgusted.

She sat on his lap, "Well, there you have it. She thought you left with that ole girl."
For obvious reasons, the information didn't make David feel any better about what happened. He felt, even if he had left with Fin-D, was it any worse than her being upstairs in a private party?

"I didn't trip on her," he reasoned.

THEY GOT GAME

Martie listened as Thaddeus explained how he couldn't explain losing his wallet with all of his money. He ran down the scenario as he remembered, retracing the events of last night, *'The six of them were at the hotel bar and each one of them bought three rounds a piece. They shot pool and played darts. They all tipped the waitress to flirt with the groom-to-be and they ended the evening by going back to the room and ordering room service.'* Thaddeus claimed the last time he remembered pulling out his wallet was when he paid for his three rounds. Martie knew it had to be more than what Thaddeus was telling her. She could feel it in her gut. She felt any guess she would make about where Thaddeus' money went, would be closer to

the truth than what he was saying. That's because
she knew Thaddeus never kept money in his wallet.
He always kept his money in his front pockets with
the smaller bills on top. That's how it was every time
she checked his pants and wallet while he slept.
Martie knew Thaddeus had three hundred dollars
when he left Beaumont to go to Houston, and she
gave him an extra hundred for an emergency. She
questioned how he figured he still had three hundred
dollars in his *wallet* after buying three rounds for six
people, ordering room service, and tipping a
waitress. Thaddeus went silent for a minute but soon
confessed that he must have lost count, saying he
must have spent more than he figured. Martie knew
he was lying through his teeth, but something kept
preventing her from calling him on it. It wasn't like
she didn't want to call him on it. She just couldn't,
and it was painful listening to him make a fool of
himself. But after accepting his apology for being
careless with the money, Martie confessed her love
and encouraged him to be safe on his way home
before hanging up. Then she just sat there, listening
to the quietness of the house. Thaddeus' lies had
created a much-needed sanctuary moment. She
started her morning over with another shower and
remoisturize herself. She started to walk through the
house wearing only her slippers, but decided to carry

her house coat with her—just in case. She poured herself a glass of red wine and took a sip before bringing the bottle with her to the back room. Martie lit a sea breeze incense and pressed play on the stereo. She stood in front of the speaker while Johnny Taylor's voice traveled up and down and all around her body, getting her in the mood. She sipped with her eyes closed and slow danced, imagining she was putty in the hands of a strong capable man. She set the volume high enough to sing with him, and low enough to hear the doorbell in case it rang. Then she reached under the sofa and pulled out the King Edward cigar box with the plastic bag full of joints she'd already rolled. She flattened the plastic bag, spreading out the joints so she could find one of the thicker ones of the bunch. After selecting one, she got comfortable on the sofa, sitting with one of her legs underneath her. She took a sip of wine and then lit up. She took a nice drag and watched the cherry brighten. Then she let the smoke billow at least an inch from her mouth before sucking it all in again. She blew and watched the stream of smoke travel across the room and disperse as it caressed the stereo receiver in front of her. She smiled—relaxed.

Martie looked at David's little boy picture on the wall. He was three years old and just as handsome as he could be, she thought. She chuckled at the memory of some of the silly things he did as a child. It was hard to believe her baby was about to be twenty-three years old. Martie took another drag and thought to call David so he could tell her something sweet, and just as she reached for the phone, it rang. She answered. It was David—calling collect. Martie quickly acccpted and excitedly prepared her heart for some of his sweet talk, but the sweetest thing David said to her was, *hey white girl.* After that, he nearly blew her high with his drama with Sydney— unloading in her ear how *he was coming home because Sydney embarrassed him. She tried to fight him. She tried to hit him, kick him, and stomp his foot with the heel of her shoe. She spit in his face—twice. Lydia tried to choke him and that he nearly got into a fight with seven guys.* On top of that, he said, *Sydney left him and he didn't even know where he was. He had to get a taxi to the hotel.* And suddenly, he had to go because his taxi had just arrived to pick him up. He promised to call her back from Sydney's. He hung up. Martie felt worse than what she did before he called—collect. Her clock read two o'clock Central Time. If she could have pressed rewind, she would have.

David's taxi arrived at Sydney's place at three-forty-five Eastern Time in that afternoon. He rang the doorbell. Lydia opened the door—inviting him in, but silently. She was barefoot and wearing volleyball shorts and a sleeveless t-shirt tied into a knot-ball at the hip.

David didn't know if Lydia was dressed as she was to provoke him to say something about her fineness, as he normally would have, but he made it clear, "I don't want any problems. I'm just here to get my stuff."

Lydia blankly stared at David, wondering why he was standing there like a stranger instead of coming in. He asked Sydney's whereabouts.

"In her room," Lydia replied.

David started, "Can you—"

Lydia interjected, "David, come in." She waved his taxi off.

David inhaled deeply before stepping inside, remaining near the door, playing it as safe as possible. Qadir's words about domestic violence charges in Georgia took the lead. He didn't want to say or do anything that could be misunderstood. Lydia made the first move, hoping he would accept her apology for putting trying to put him in a chokehold. She said she really didn't want to get involved, but she thought he was about to fight Sydney, and as a friend, she couldn't just let that happen. David said everything was cool, and nothing else. Lydia wanted to apologize for her misreading the situation that sent things off the rails, but she could tell David had nothing for her. He wouldn't even look at her. She stood near him long enough for the awkward silence to sound like a scream, and when it did, she made a slow about-face and walked away, into Sydney's room. David trotted up the stairs to his room and started getting his things together. He was taking things out of the dresser drawers when Sydney abruptly walked into the room. She closed the door and locked it. For a moment, she stood there, looking like she had a bad cold—red nose and puffy eyes.

"What?" David asked, defensively.

Sydney squeezed her interlocked fingers. Her knuckles cracked. She sighed, "David, I'm sorry. I thought you left with that girl…and…what can I say? I lost it. I was hurt. I was embarrassed."

David shook his head, "No, Syd…I ain't buying it. You did not do that because you thought I left with some female. Especially after you spent all that time upstairs with Rich. Nah…"
Sydney grabbed two handfuls of her hair and squeezed. "Ok. First, Lydia told me that she saw you and Tasha coming out of a room together and that y'all disappeared. I lost it. I couldn't think. Everything kind of went crazy from there. We looked for y'all. I found Tasha. She was drunk, and

crying about you, saying she let you down and that you were disappointed in her. I thought she was saying something happened between y'all and I was about to get in her ass. If it wasn't for Lydia, I would have. I remember asking her where you were and she said you left with that girl that you were cozied up with. That's when she told me what happened, that the girl you left with had walked in on her and a guy in the bathroom."

"So, at first you thought I messed with Tasha?" David questioned.

"Yes," she whispered, "But only because…," she paused, and confessed, "David, everything was just crazy."
Sydney tried to explain how she misunderstood what actually happened. Then she backtracked, saying, in her heart, she knew nothing happened between him and Tasha. She didn't really believe he would do something like that. She admitted to not having the same confidence with him leaving with a female. So, when she saw him a whole hour later, after dealing with her rollercoaster of emotions, she exploded. Sydney tried to hug David, but he didn't want it. She aggressively pursued the hug while David carefully avoided resisting harshly. He asked her to let him go. She wouldn't. He stood still. Hands at his side while Sydney's face was buried against his chest.

Eventually, he pried himself loose, claiming he needed her to look at him. He wanted to know something. She loosened her hold and looked him in the eyes.

He asked, "What were you doing up there?" Sydney promised that all she and Rich did was talk inside of his studio. She said she played some tunes on the piano and they talked about working together.

David's voice trembled when he asked, "So, you want me to believe that's all you did upstairs where a sex and drug party was going on?"

"Yes, I want you to believe what I'm telling you. I wasn't up there for all of that. The only thing that happened is what I told you. I promise," Sydney claimed.

Disgusted by Sydney's avoidance, David turned and started stuffing his things into his bag. Sydney felt the disconnection, still she asked what he was doing, though she clearly saw and understood that he was packing to leave.

"I'm going home," he replied. He continued stuffing his bag.

"Wait a minute. David, wait. Stop. Stop. Stop David!" She insisted.

Sydney grabbed his arm to make him stop but when he jerked away from her. This provoked Sydney to grab him more firmly, demanding he stop and talk to her.

David sighed. Almost whispering, he said, "I just…want to go home."

"Why? Because of a disagreement?"

Hurt, with tears forming, David blasted, "Syd! That was not a disagreement! You jumped on me. You spit in my face, twice. Then you left me surrounded by niggas who were getting ready to hurt me. That's not a disagreement, Syd."

"David, please don't leave like this. Let me make this right."

David understood where Sydney's mind was headed with her idea of making it right. That was her quick fix to a big problem. Though intense and extremely pleasurable, Sydney's make-up sex was a hard resist, but considering his recklessness with Marjorie just hours ago, he couldn't go there with her—not even with a condom. Instead, he invited his friend to sit down so she could hear his heart. David asked Sydney if she remembered what happened when they were eleven, right after they returned from their summer vacations.

"A lot of stuff happened back then," Sydney painfully remembered.

"True," David acknowledged, "But that was the first time you hit me. You pushed me in my face and you screamed at me, telling me not to touch you. You grabbed my shirt and tried to sling me to the ground and when I didn't fall, you hit me in the back with your fist."

David painfully admitted, what had happened at Rich's house the night before reminded him of that traumatizing moment when they were kids. When it happened back then, he ran home to his mom, but when Sydney left him as she did, he felt abandoned by the one person he loved most.

"David…" she interjected.

"No, no…just hear me out," David said, refusing to let his tears fall. "I felt like I was in a bad spot," he said. After a long pause, David continued, "Syd, your life has changed…and it's about to change even more with this music stuff. You're already busy…and now you're gonna be flying everywhere, meeting all kinds of people…" David sighed, "You're not gonna have time for me…and I can't compete with what you have going on."

Affectionately, Sydney replied, "David, I will always have time for you. You're my best friend," she persuaded.

"I'm your best friend?" David questioned.

Sydney affirmed, "Yes, you're my best friend, and I'm asking my best friend not to leave. Especially not like this."

"Syd, I'm going home."

"Can you at least give me until Monday, Tuesday, or even Wednesday? Please?" she begged. Monday was Sydney's birthday and her mom was flying in on Tuesday. Wednesday was the AKA-sponsored birthday party at the Peachtree Westin Plaza, and Friday was Sydney's official release party hosted by Solara Records. David had come to Alpharetta to attend all of those events. What Sydney had planned for his birthday was still a secret, but after a few moments of silence and strong eye-to-eye contact, he agreed to stay only until Wednesday, but it wasn't for her alone. He thought his staying a few extra days was a courtesy for the time and space he shared with Marjorie. However, the remainder of that Saturday was very stale. Tasha, Lydia and Sydney talked to one another and even left the condo to go somewhere. David showered and then talked with his mom on the phone for nearly an hour, and with Marjorie for a few moments when she called to check on him. Sunday, David and Aaron went to Cumberland Mall so he could buy Sydney's birthday gift. He bought her a perfume and lotion set—Ysatis, by Givenchy. When he discovered the fragrance he smelled at Marjorie's brother's condo was Egyptian Musk, he bought several bottles of the body oil for himself. Aaron's main purpose for going to the mall was to flirt, and possibly pick up a female or two, which he did not fail in doing. Aaron's conversation revolved around women, sex, and his desires for any attractive woman. It made for a long evening. When they arrived at Sydney's at seven o'clock that evening, David's heart dropped when he saw Marjorie's white BMW parked out front. He didn't expect to see her so soon, especially not at Sydney's, and especially without his planning how to handle their in-person interaction since their encounter. His mind raced, wondering how to handle such an awkward moment of seeing her and Sydney in the same room. Aaron didn't make the moment too comfortable either. He didn't know Marjorie, but he'd seen her before. He asked if the BMW belonged to a slim chick with nice breasts—describing them by holding his clawed hands at least five inches from his chest. He lusted, describing what he thought the color and shape of her nipples might be. David laughed. Aaron was spot on, but David didn't let him know he was right. That would have only hyped Aaron up, and David had had enough sex talk for one day.

David opened the car door to get out, but Aaron told him to wait a minute. He told him to close the door because he wanted to ask him something.

Aaron appeared to be thinking about something serious.

"What's up, man?" David asked, concerned.

Aaron stuttered, "Hey, hey uh…your girl. You say y'all just friends, right?"

Nigga, don't you dare ask me to hook you up with Syd, David thought, before answering, "Yeah, man. We've been friends since we were babies…so be careful what you say to me about her," he warned.

"Nah, nah, nah…ain't, ain't, nuthin crazy or nuthin. A brother, a brother just want to know…how you do that? How do you be around a female as fine as she is and just be friends with her?" he inquired.

Agitated, David smacked, "Man…"

"Seriously man. I know at some point you had to see her naked…or at least half naked…or something. The last time you were here it was just y'all two in the house. I know you got to be hittin that, huh?"

Agitated, David sighed, "Look man, Syd is my friend…she's always been a friend, and it ain't that kind of party. I know too much about her to be trying to deal with her like that…you know? Hell, sometimes that girl is like my sister…other times she's like my homeboy…we've always been that way," David explained.

Aaron claimed he understood and that he respected what David said, but David could see something in Aaron's eyes that didn't look right. Aaron's complete silence didn't feel right—it was awkward at best. David asked if everything was all right. Aaron shook his head slowly, saying everything wasn't all right. He looked as if a ton of bricks had been dropped on him, before mentioning he had a friend. He paused like he wasn't sure if he should say what he was thinking, and decided to act like what he was thinking wasn't too important. He just reached over to give David a pound, and a fist bump and admitted that him having a homegirl that he could just be cool with was a good thing.

"Don't ever mess that up…real talk. Don't ever mess that up," Aaron repeated.

"For sho," David answered, before stepping out of the car and watching Aaron as he drove off. Before going inside David put on his game face. He walked onto the porch and stood at the door. He took a deep breath, let it out, inserted his key, and opened the door. The ladies were in the living room and where Marjorie was sitting, she was the first one David saw when he walked in.

He spoke to everyone as he handed Sydney the small, decorated bag, "Happy Birthday," he said.

Sydney's eyes lit up. She stood up to hug and thank him before taking the bag. She knew it had to be perfume. It was no secret that David loved a good-smelling woman. It was his thing, so she knew whatever the fragrance was, it was something he thought would smell delicious on her. In his normal way and despite the lingering tension, David made his way around the room. He greeted Tasha with a hug and kiss on the cheek. He went to Lydia who cut her eyes up at him as if she was warning him, but he kissed her cheek anyway. She let him. When it was Marjorie's turn she stood up for a real hug. They embraced and kissed each other's cheeks. Marjorie allowed her hands to travel down David's back as they released their hug. The gesture pinched Sydney's emotions. David went upstairs and it was nine o'clock when he returned wearing cutoff warm-up bottoms and a wife beater. Marjorie was just about to leave, but when she saw David's fine shoulders and smelled the fragrance from her brother's condo, she lingered, knowing David was communicating with her.

She flirted, "Mr. Caramel with cocoa-buttered skin…all the way down to his toes."

"Girl…cocoa butter on everything," Sydney replied.

The two felines laughed but David corrected them. "Pond's Cold Cream on it first. Sometimes Noxzema. Gotta keep it extra clean," he said.

Marjorie burst out laughing and Sydney chimed in, "And he's serious too. He takes care of that thang."

"And he should," Marjorie replied. "Because it ain't nothing worse than smelling some old musty balls."

Sydney screamed, laughing. Marjorie asked, pausing to make a stink face, as if she relived the moment, "Girl…did I tell you about that time?" She mentioned.

"Yes, you did," Sydney answered, laughing so hard she was about to choke.

Marjorie shook her head, "Just musty. Just stank. So, yea, keep it clean brother man…you never know when a chick might wanna kiss it," she said, before calling it a night.

Sydney walked Marjorie out, intending to watch her leave, but Marjorie invited Sydney to get some distance away from her door to ensure a little privacy. She wanted to ask her something.

Sydney followed her, "What's up?"

Marjorie sucked her teeth, before purring, devilishly, "Soooo…are you sharing?"

"Sharing what?" Sydney asked, curiously.

Marjorie gave a head and eye gesture towards Sydney's front door.

Sydney looked back towards her front door and asked again, "What?"

"Your boy," Marjorie answered.

"David? No," Sydney snapped. "And by the way, I saw how you rubbed my man's back when you hugged him earlier…don't make me break your lil fingers okay?"

"Oh, so he's your man now?" Marjorie pried.

"While he's here he is," Sydney answered, smirking.

"So, you're holding out on your big sister?" Marjorie dug.

"Marjorie, you know how I feel about David."

"And you knew how I felt about Terrence too," Marjorie reminded.

"Marjorie, you did not care about Terrence. Furthermore, what happened that night was your plan. You wanted to play that blindfold game with him," Sydney reminded.

"But you laid up there and enjoyed it…didn't you?" Marjorie charged.

"What was I supposed to do?" Sydney asked, chuckling.

Emphatically, Marjorie replied, "The same thing I want to do to David."

"No. You can have Lilo," Sydney offered.

"Girl, you don't even want Lilo. I heard that thing is curved like a boomerang anyway," Marjorie answered with a frown.

Sydney laughed, admitting it was, which is why she was offering him, "Furthermore, you wouldn't enjoy David anyway," Sydney squeaked, sizing David with her little finger.

"Girl please," Marjorie snapped, "I know brother man is packing."

"What do you mean you know?" Sydney barked.

Marjorie wished she could say what she already knew for a fact, but safely answered, "That print. I saw the print in those jeans baby," Marjorie admitted.

Sydney frowned, but Marjorie smiled, waiting for the green light to spend some time with David. Marjorie reminded Sydney that if it wasn't for her the two of them would not be getting along right now, and that David would probably be back in Texas.

Sydney agreed, but bluntly answered, "No. Not him. He's off-limits."

"Sis…you know the rule. He's not your man. He's never been your man. Those are your words. Remember?" Marjorie reminded. "Plus, I don't want him for my man. I just want him for a moment. You can have him back when I'm done."

"Marjorie, don't do this. Not him," Sydney pleaded. "If the shoe was on the other foot, what would you do? Really?" Sydney questioned.

"I would give my sister what she's asking for, but that's me," Marjorie answered, before reaching for a hug.

Sydney reluctantly hugged Marjorie back. They kissed each other's cheek before saying goodnight.

Sydney went back inside and went straight to David's room. The first thing she did was bury her face in his neck, smelling his fragrance, "That really smells good. What is it called?"

"Egyptian Musk," David answered.

Bluntly, Sydney asked David if he would tell her if any of her friends tried to come on to him. David answered Sydney's question with the same question. She answered, saying she would, so David replied he would.

"So, you wouldn't tell me if you didn't think I would tell you?" Sydney questioned.

"Nope," David answered.

DYSFUNCTION

David moved his things into Tasha's room so Sydney's mom could have her own space when she came. Her plane was arriving at one-thirty in the afternoon on Sydney's birthday. Sydney had taken it upon herself and planned for David to go with her and Lydia to the training facility, and grab a quick lunch afterwards, before heading to the airport to get her mom. David had plans for a haircut and lunch with Aaron, who was paying. Sydney managed to keep her peace about his plans but she was upset about David making personal plans for her birthday. She wanted them to hang out together all day but because he had other plans, she suggested, as she had once before, for him to take Tasha with him. She wished to interrupt any additional plans he and Aaron might have had.

"You do know Aaron drives a Vette, right?" David reminded. "Why don't you take her with you?"

"Then take the Jetta," Sydney answered with a slight attitude.

Offended, Tasha interjected, "Whoa, whoa, whoa…ain't nobody gotta take me nowhere. Especially if neither one of y'all want to have anything to do with me."

"Nah boo. It's not like that," David assured, "You can hang out with me anytime. It was just that Aaron was treating me to a haircut and lunch."

"On my birthday! My birthday!" Sydney replied, before roughly snatching her keys off of the counter and heading to the garage.

David called Aaron to get an update on the time they were heading out. The barbershop they were going to was about a forty-five-minute drive. Daddy D'z BBQ was about ten minutes from the barbershop, so Aaron planned on heading out no later than eleven. That gave David enough time to treat Tasha to breakfast at the Original Pancake House. It was the first time they had a moment together since the Friday night madness. They talked about the bathroom incident. Tasha admitted that it could have easily been him several times since being in Georgia.

As tempting as that sounded, David admitted he couldn't have gone there with her, "And it's not because you're Sydney's cousin either," David admitted. "Well, it is one of the reasons, but even if you were one of her friends, I couldn't do that in that girl's house. Don't get me wrong, like I said before, I do have a thing for thick pretty girls"

His attempt to boost Tasha's self-esteem in the moment, worked. She smiled. As embarrassed as she had been with David knowing what had happened, she was glad he didn't see it happening. Plus, his continued friendship despite her bad judgment meant the world to her. By the time they'd finished their pancakes, eggs, and grits, everything was starting to feel normal again. Their hug and David's kiss on her forehead before leaving with Aaron, reaffirmed their friendship. For the first time, Tasha truly felt respected by a man who not only said he cared about her but showed her he did. After their haircuts, while on their way to Daddy D'z Barbeque Joynt, Aaron confessed that they were meeting up with a couple of females. If everything went as planned, Aaron would be at the hotel and David would have to make a few long blocks around the area before coming back to get him.

"That is if you're not next door knocking one of them down yourself," he said—overly excited.
As Aaron said, a few females, four of them exactly, were at the barbeque restaurant waiting. Three of them looked about college-age, but one of them looked like she could have been the cool auntie. The cool auntie seemed familiar with Aaron and took a quick interest in David too—asking what he did for a living. It took all of ten seconds talking with her for David to pick up on what was going on. It was almost as if Ara had fed him the information

telepathically from over 800 miles away, Auntie was pushing a product, and those females were money girls—probably college students making tuition money. David didn't even want to know their names, because he wasn't buying what they were selling. Aaron was all in like Flynn. David dropped him off at a nearby hotel to meet the three women. Aaron told him to be back in an hour, but after that hour, David still had to wait an extra thirty minutes. Aaron came out looking relieved. The only question David asked him, was if he was good. He said he was, but for the first time since David had met Aaron, he was rather quiet, with the exception of giving directions back to Sydney's. Fifteen minutes into the ride home, Aaron picked up where he left off on a previous conversation. He asked again about being able to be a friend with a woman without crossing the line; and if lines were crossed, how would he know if the friend's no, really means no?

David replied, with serious wonder, "I'm not following dawg."

"Man, I'm sure you know how uh…you know when friends just be playing around and things kinda go there. It's like she asks you what you doing, but you know it's what both of y'all been hinting around to. You and your girl been there, right?" Aaron asked.

David asked, seeking clarity, "You mean, like me trying to get at her, and she ain't with it?

"Not that serious, but sort of," Aaron answered, timidly.

In his mind, David was asking what went on in that hotel room, but with his mouth, he stuck with the friendship story of him and Sydney.

"Look bruh, me and Syd are friends. Friends. She's a good-looking woman…always has been, but we're just close. I mean, I don't know what else to tell you," David answered, hoping to squash that topic.

Aaron sank back into silence until they pulled up in front of Sydney's townhome at ten minutes after five. They both got out and met at the back of the car. They gave each other dap with the shoulder bump. David thanked him for the cut and lunch. As he did before, David stood on the walkway and watched Aaron drive off before going inside.

He walked inside, declaring, "I don't want to see nobody or talk to anybody…until I see my baby. All I wanna do…is see my baby."

DeDe immediately started laughing, knowing David was talking about her. David fake sprinted to the kitchen area, but was intercepted by Sydney because of his haircut. It was different. He had a high, bald fade.

"Who cut your hair? Sydney asked, looking amazed.

"A dude they call Flip over at the Chop Shop," David answered, before side-stepping her to get to her mom.

David fake stumbled into the kitchen—grabbing his chest. DeDe had just put the finishing touch on her gumbo. She was on the phone with Martie, complaining about the grocery stores in Georgia not having her type of sausage and no smoked turkey necks.

David rushed to DeDe and bear hugged her, kissing her cheek repeatedly as she tensed and laughed aloud, telling him, "Move boy…looking mo an mo like that Larry Jr.," she said.

She was telling him to move, but she never tried to get out of David's grasp. She teased Martie, saying she was over there getting all of her son's kisses.

She handed him the phone, "Yere boy, thas yo mama on da phone."

David took the phone, "Hey white girl…whatchu mean don't hey you?" David asked.

"Tell huh don't be gettin jealous," DeDe teased.

"Yea, don't be getting jealous," David continued, "You know I love you…yes, I do…and I miss you too…then I tell you what…I'll just have to give you some extra kisses when I come home…yea…that's right…ok…who's there?" David asked, as he walked out of the kitchen.

Marjorie looked surprised by how David gushed over the phone. She whispered to Sydney and asked if he was really talking to his mama like that, and Sydney whispered back, that it was, adding that he'd always been that way with his mama.

"That is so cute," Marjorie expressed

"Hmph. So, says the girl who hates mama's boys," Sydney replied, twisting her lips.

David continued his conversation with his mom, asking who was at the house and why she was trying to get off the phone all of a sudden.

"Ha, ha, ha, nothing. Who is that?" David questioned. "Quit fibbing woman. That is not Mr. Chasion…Put him on the phone…if it's Mr. Chasion, then put him on the phone….if it is Mr. Chasion he would want to speak to me…because he told me he would have some plums for me when I got back…then put him on the phone…then tell him to say something…yes, say something because I know how he sounds…I don't believe you woman…because you're laughing…no, I'm not jealous…I'm not jealous…then put him on the phone. Hey Mr. Chasion…yes sir…yes

sir…Wednesday…yes sir… all right…see you when I get back." After a long pause, David ended his conversation, "Yea woman, of course…I'm not sure how much is in there, but it should be enough for that…if not, I can tell Piggy to get it from my apartment and bring it to you tomorrow…yes ma'am…I love you too."
David hung up with his mom, and did his usual, making his way around to each person, greeting them with a hug and kiss. Everyone ate, and Marjorie left. The next morning DeDe cooked breakfast—pancakes, eggs, sausage, and grits for herself, David, and Tasha. She made a fruit salad for Sydney and Lydia before they left heading to the training facility. David planned to eat after his morning jog but when he returned, he walked into the house disturbed. He'd just seen Aaron being led to a police car in handcuffs. Aaron's neighbor said he was arrested and charged with rape.

"Some girl he knows says he raped her," David repeated, realizing, that's what had to be on Aaron's mind.

When Sydney returned home and found out what happened to Aaron, she flew into a rage, asking, but almost accusing David of being a part of whatever happened with Aaron, "You were with him! What did you do? What happened? Were you with him when it happened?" Sydney investigated, nervously. David couldn't answer, because he didn't know when the supposed rape happened. All he could think about was dropping Aaron off at the hotel. He recounted to Sydney, and everyone standing around waiting for an answer, what happened when he left with Aaron. They went to the Chop Shop and then to Daddy D'z Joynt where Aaron had met some females.

"Oh, where Aaron met some females! Like you didn't meet some females," Sydney barked, still breathing hard.

"No, I didn't meet any females. I mean, I met them because Aaron paid for everyone's food. We were sitting together, but when we all left, I dropped Aaron off at the hotel and went back to get him after about an hour and a half," David answered. Frustrated by the skeptical looks, he was getting, he yelled, "I didn't do nothing!"

"David, you better not be lying. I swear! I don't need this bull crap. My life and my career are too important to be anywhere near this kind of stuff" Sydney exclaimed, as worry began to wear on her face.

"Syd! Don't you think if I was a part of anything Aaron did, the police would be here now? Hell, I was right there when they were putting him in the car."

Sydney turned and walked into her room and slammed her door shut. The silence was deafening but David stood there with a mixture of rage and embarrassment, feeling like Sydney had placed a sign over his head that read: *'Lowlife Sicko.'* No one said another word. Two hours had passed when the event was reported on the news, and by evening, more information had been released. The incident in question was reported by a woman who claimed to have been a friend of Aaron's, who said he assaulted her four months prior. Factually, David was vindicated—he wasn't anywhere near Aaron when it happened. He wasn't even in Georgia. Emotionally, David felt like he'd been disemboweled, and his guts were still on the floor. No one apologized for their assumptions and perceptions of him, and he was too hurt to celebrate the truth coming to light.

***

Martie woke up thinking about Louise. Thinking about Louise wasn't unusual, but the feeling in Martie's heart for Louise was unusual. She felt a sense of sorrow—like Louise was missing something she needed. The feeling wouldn't budge from Martie's gut, so she eventually gave in and called to check on her. Louise answered the phone with her usual greeting,

"Praise da Lawd."

"Hey, mama. Whatchu doin'?"

"Nothin Martha Louise…whatchu want?" Louise's tone was as sharp as a razor and it made Martie immediately snap back,

"Nothing. I just called to see how you were doing."

"Well, I'm doin' fine," Louise answered, but then remained silent, holding the phone.
Martie held the phone in silence for a few seconds, regretting she even called to check on the old hellcat. Louise remained silent on the other end, aggravated because Martie wasn't saying anything. Marty broke the silence,

"Mama, why do you hate me?"

"Lawd Jesus, Martha Louise. Don't botha me wit dis nah…I ain't got time fuh dis."

"Well, me neither mama. I really just called to check on you but you act like I just ruined your day…like you hate me."

"Whoo, Lawd Hammurcy Jesus dis chile. Martha, why yu call me wit dis early dis moanin?"

"You want me to call you later and ask the same question?"

"Gul…is yu crazy? Have yu lost yu mind Martha? Nah, da only-is reesun yu call me nah is becuz yu miss dat woman. Otha wise yu wudn't be studdin bout me. If I don't come to yu house, yu don't even thank to come by yere," Louise snapped, hurt.

"Mama that is not true. Every time I try to talk to you this is what you do. You talk to me like you hate me. You act like you blame me for everything that goes wrong."

"Ooh…Lawd," Louise replied, agitated.

"Bye mama."

Martie slammed the phone in Louise's ear and sat up in the bed for a moment, before deciding to go to the bathroom. Martie stared at her pale face in the mirror, looking tired and sad too. At thirty-eight years old, Martie felt like she was getting old. She sighed and grabbed the jar of Pond's cold cream. She cleaned, rinsed, and dried her face. She felt like it made a difference. She looked a little better. Then she inspected other areas of what she thought was evidence of an aging body—pressing, lifting, squeezing and looking at her reflection in the full-body mirror. She decided to encourage herself, telling herself she still looked good, especially for a woman with a soon to be twenty-three-year-old. *'Where has the time gone?'* She thought to herself.

Martie went about doing busy work in the house. Nothing really needed to be done, she just needed to occupy her mind, but she kept looking at the phone, thinking she should give it another try. She did. She called Louise and Louise answered again, with her usual greeting.

"Let's try this again. Hey Mama."
Martie heard Louise mumble something, and it might as well had been as though Louise had stuck Martie in the behind with a hot iron. She immediately wanted to cuss Louise, but instead, she asked Louise a question that she didn't even know she wanted to ask. It just came out.

"Mama, how is it that you love my daddy so much, but seem to hate his child?"

"Lawd Je-sus Martha…yu gon give me a heart attack gul…stop dis…dis ain't nuthin but da devil in yu."

"I ain't got no devil…but will you *please*…answer my question," Martie demanded.
Once again Louise just held the phone in silence. Martie held the phone in silence. A few minutes passed with only a couple of sighs between the two until Martie blurted,

"I met my aunt Edna a while back."

"What Martha?" Louise asked, still agitated.

"My Aunt Edna. I met her when I went to the funeral in Ville Platte. Why you never told me my daddy had sisters and a brother?"

"Gul, I dun kno no Edna…I dun kno yu daddy people…"

"Well, she said all y'all worked for Frank Duplichin when y'all were teenagers."
Martie continued sharing with Louise the things she remembered Edna telling her, but as she talked, she heard a dial tone. Louise had hung up on her and then wouldn't answer the phone when Martie called back.

"Old hateful ass," Martie gritted, before slamming the phone down.
Martie picked up the phone again and started punching in Larry Jr.'s number, but when she put the phone to her ear, David was on the line, yelling,

"Hello!"
Confused, Martie questioned,

"David…what are you…why are you on the…where are you at?"

"I'm in Georgia. I just called you and you picked up the phone punching numbers in my ear. Who were you calling all fast like that?" David asked.
Martie quickly settled her emotions the best she could and greeted David with her usual greeting, but ignored his question. He asked again, who she was

calling. But she smacked and told him he was being awfully nosey.

"Yep. Just like my mama," David answered.

"I miss you," Martie confessed, avoiding the question again. "I thought you forgot about your mama. I ain't heard from you since you left." David smacked,

"Woman, I just talked to you last night."

"Are you sure? Cuz, I don't remember that," Martie joked.

"Yeah…you couldn't sleep because you were still upset about Thaddeus being at a bachelor's party."

"Men's night out," Martie corrected.

"Mama, you know that was a bachelor's party with strippers," David teased. Martie replied, in her Creole accent´,

"Chile…I ain't wurrid bout Thad an no strippas. Thas you wit dem strippas…"

"Whatever man…"

"And you gon stop calling me man. Do I look like a man to you?" Martie fussed.

"Whatever woman. Is Thaddeus there?"

"No. He's still at work."

"So, y'all made up?"

"I'm fine," Martie claimed, "He keeps asking me what's wrong, but I guess that's his guilt."

The doorbell rang, and when Martie saw that it was Earnest, she tried to get off the phone, but David wouldn't let her because he needed to talk.

"I'm coming…give me just a moment!" Martie yelled, before telling David again she had to go.

"Mama!" David yelled.

"What boy?"

"Who is that?" David asked.

"Why?" Martie teased.

David sighed and asked if Piggy was still at the house. Martie told him she wasn't, that she had left yesterday. Frustrated, David tried to get his mom's attention again, but she was too busy playing, and it was aggravating David something serious until he just blurted out that he was coming home early. Martie suddenly became concerned, asking,

"What's wrong baby?"

David answered, saying, "Long story. Love you, bye."

Before Martie could return the love, David had already hung up. Martie gave Earnest her attention. She offered to fix him breakfast, but he settled for a cup of coffee. Martie put some coffee on and went ahead and fixed Earnest a plate from her leftovers—smothered steak, black-eyed peas, and a few yams so he could eat later. Martie fixed Earnest's cup of coffee the way he liked it—black with two sugar cubes. She fixed hers—adding coffee to her four sugar cubes and cream. The two sat and talked for a good while, and before Earnest decided it was time to leave, he reached into his pocket and pulled out a leather key ring, with two keys on it. Martie's heart thumped, knowing the keys were to the Mustang.

"So, you're finally ready to sell it?" Martie asked, excitedly.

"No," Earnest answered. "But I am ready to give it to someone I truly appreciate."
Martie reached past the keys for Earnest. He wrapped his long slender arm around Martie's shoulders and thanked her for every kind act she'd shown him over the years. It almost sounded like he was going somewhere and it made Martie squeeze Earnest even tighter. She couldn't thank him enough and she wanted to give him something. David had already given her the money for the car. She had the full payment, but Earnest wouldn't accept a penny. He only expected her to say she bought it if anyone asked. Thaddeus made it home about an hour after the transaction, and seeing the white Mustang parked out front, he couldn't get himself situated fast enough, before hurrying into the house, wondering why Earnest was there. Thaddeus looked as if he stumbled into the house, looking wild-eyed, as if he was expecting to see something wrong or

questionable. But Martie was sitting at the dining room table going through a bunch of junk and papers she'd cleaned out of her Cordoba. She was still overjoyed with her new car, but it didn't take long before Thaddeus called it a bad decision. Going backward from 1978 to 1966 didn't make much sense to him. Never mind the car being a complete cherry, which is what Earnest called it. Martie attempted to explain how the car was all original with only fifteen thousand original miles.

"Earnest kept that car in the garage even before his wife died. That car is immaculate and it runs like a sewing machine." Martie defended.
Still, Thaddeus insisted she twist that deal and get her money back. Martie defended her decision, saying David bought that car for her, and that started another argument along with one hundred and two more questions. But for a man who lost three hundred dollars, Thaddeus had his nerves questioning Martie about her and David's real financial status. Her answer was the same as it was when he first asked about how she takes care of herself. She repeated, how Black was a terrible husband, but was smart enough to have decent life insurance policies, and life insurance on everything he was making payments on. Everything was paid off. Thaddeus didn't like the way Martie was

snapping her answers and argued back with her—
yelling at her, but he shut his mouth when she
reminded him of how he enjoyed everything in that
house without paying for any of it.

"Now, my son gave me the money to buy that car.
I bought the car, and I'm keeping the car!" She
yelled.

Take Care

It was 4:30 in the morning when David went
upstairs to Tasha's room to get his things, and to tell
her bye. He sat on the edge of the bed and quietly
woke her up. She thought she was dreaming. She
thought it was David by the voice, but it was dark
and her eyes were trying to focus. He'd come to tell
her bye. Tasha quickly raised, with concern and
asked,

"Where are you going?"
David whispered that he was going to the airport,
and Tasha quickly wrapped her arms around him,
confessing she wished he would stay, but strangely,
she understood why he was leaving. Things hadn't
been right since Friday night. She asked if he might

visit Baton Rouge any time soon and if he would remember her number if she gave it to him. She wanted him to call her sometime, and to keep in touch. He promised he would remember it. She gave him her grandmother's number and David repeated it, tapping on his temple to let her know he had it locked in. He kissed Tasha's forehead and told her to be good to herself, before leaving without telling anyone else he was leaving—defeated. Tasha could feel him and when everyone else woke up, they could feel something was different too. Sydney assumed David had gone for his jog, and DeDe fixed an amount of breakfast that included David, but Tasha chose not to say anything until someone asked about him. When Sydney finally noticed her house key on the stand in the foyer, wonder traveled across her face, but she didn't say anything right then. A few moments later she went upstairs and looked in Tasha's room and bathroom, and when she didn't see David's bags or essentials, she hurried back downstairs and asked if anyone had talked with David.

"He's gone," Tasha answered.

"What do you mean, gone?" Sydney questioned.

"Gone, as in, he left…gone."

"Where?"

"Home," Tasha explained.

Sydney's heart sank and all her insides felt like they gathered into a ball.

"Why? When did he leave?" Sydney asked. Tasha didn't know, but she knew it was early. Sydney sent David a series of 911 pages, forgetting his Texas pager didn't work while in Georgia, which is why he was using hers. She called his mom to see if she talked with him. She did. She said David was at the airport getting his flight changed. Martie asked what was going on and Sydney just called it a misunderstanding. She promised to tell her later. Sydney hung up and called Continental to check their flights to Houston. There was one leaving in twenty minutes and another leaving at ten thirty. The lady confirmed David as a passenger on the ten-thirty flight, and Sydney requested that David be notified of an emergency. In a nervous fit Sydney was about to leave the house in shorts and slippers. She would have if her mom hadn't intervened, telling her she better put on some clothes. Sydney quickly slid into a pair of running pants and she and Lydia left, hoping to catch David in time, but she ran into dead-stop highway traffic. She screamed! Meanwhile, David was headed to his gate, but decided to call Mr. Sammy to let him know he was coming back early. Mrs. Mary accepted the charges, knowing her husband would be glad to hear from David. She called Sammy to the phone,

"Pug! Pug! (Sammy's nickname) David is on the phone."
Sammy looked up from underneath the hood of his old truck.

His face was already dripping in sweat, "What's that honey?" He questioned.

"It's David," she said, holding the phone receiver so he could see it.

Sammy wiped his face with his rag and came inside to answer the phone, "Hey, long lost fella, you made it back?... Oh, you still in Atlanta?…ok, at the airport…what time you gettin in?…about twelve thirty…you got a ride?...Ok…so I guess I'll see you when you get home…that girl sure miss her brother…does she know you coming back early?… then, I won't tell her…ok, son…bye now."

Sammy hung up with a big smile on his face, "I sure did miss that fella. It seems like it's already been more than a month," he expressed.
Mary was wearing a frown as she looked at him pouring with sweat. Sammy asked what was bothering her, and she replied, he was bothering her. She'd already asked him to leave that old truck alone until it cooled off, but he just had to go mess with it anyway. Mary took Sammy's rag to wipe the sweat

off the back of his neck and the sides of his face. Not wanting to agitate Mary any further, Sammy agreed to do what she asked, before acting like he was going to hug her with his sweaty shirt and oily hands.

She screamed, "No Pug!" As she arms to turn away from him.
Sammy laughed and puckered for a kiss instead. She obliged him with a smack on the lips, before reminding she needed to pick up a few things from the grocery store as early as possible, but that she would be just a little longer than usual. Before she left, she asked him to freshen up and relax, and he promised he would after pouring himself a glass of iced tea. Mary had been gone for about two hours before returning home. When she pulled into the driveway, the hood on Sammy's old truck was still up and his tools were still out. She tooted the horn for him to come out and help with the bags, but when he didn't come, she grabbed two bags and went inside. From the side door, Mary could see Sammy sitting in his recliner.

She called to him, "Pug honey, I have a few more bags in the car."
Mary walked into the kitchen and set the bags on the kitchen table. She waited a few seconds before calling his name again. She thought maybe he'd

fallen asleep. She went as far as the door entrance leading into the den,

"Pug…I'm home," she said.
She expected Sammy to get and come to kiss her like he always does as if he was seeing her for the first time that day. When Sammy didn't answer, Mary's legs felt weak. She immediately clutched her stomach. In the forty-two years they'd been married Sammy had never slept that hard. Fear suddenly gripped Mary in the center of her chest. It reached up and tightened around her throat. She had to brace herself as she walked through the doorway into the den. When she slowly approached Sammy, she noticed the glass of iced tea spilled onto his lap. Her knees hit the floor,

"Pug! No!" Mary cried out.
Sammy's eyes were half open, but when Mary touched his face, she knew he was gone. She knew he was gone by the swelling in the sides of his neck. Mary cried briefly before getting mad at him again for working in that heat. Then she got mad at him for falling asleep in that old sweaty, dirty T-shirt. She'd always made sure he had clean clothes. She worried that the ambulance people would see him in dirty clothes. Mary quickly cleaned her husband's face and hands with a soapy towel. She covered the

wet spot from the iced tea with a towel. She was cleaning his fingernails when the ambulance arrived.

***

David arrived at Houston Hobby Airport at two fifteen. His pager was alerting non-stop with the pages he was sent while he was in flight. Most were from Sydney, or at least from Sydney's house phone and truck phone. David immediately called Mr. Sammy to tell him he had just arrived, but no one answered. He called Piggy's dorm, but she wasn't there. He called Ara's apartment to let her know he was back early, but no one answered. Ara's apartment. He called the club. She was there. He let her know he was back and that he'd bought a few things for Junior. She asked what he bought her, and he told her.

"A bag of rocks," he said, laughing.

"I'll take them too…all of'em," Ara answered, before requesting he call her later because she had something to tell him.

On his way to baggage claim, he saw a familiar face smiling at him from behind a pair of sunshades. Martie was wearing a sky-blue sundress with matching sandals. The sandals had a daisy on each foot. David smiled when he saw her because she looked rather cute,

"Aww suki suki nah…look at-chu."

"Hey, handsome," Martie replied, opening her arms for a big hug.

David and Martie hugged, rocking from side to side before smacking lips. Some of the onlookers displayed some suspicion, perhaps wondering why this white woman was so elated, hugging and kissing a young black stud. Black females couldn't hide some of the snarls on their faces, and even some white men couldn't hide their facial expressions of disdain for seeing what appeared to be a good, wholesome white woman carrying on as Martie was. Others passed on as if they hadn't seen anything. Such attitudes had always bothered David, but Martie had just learned how to ignore it—especially when she was married to a man as dark-skinned as Black was. After David retrieved his bag, he and Martie walked hand in hand to her car. When David saw the car, he complimented her, saying it looked like it was meant to be hers. They were a perfect fit—a white girl with a white car with a red interior. Martie was so happy with her car that she could hardly contain herself. She had to show David everything about her car that he already knew, and driving it with that top-down, Martie was poetry in motion. Of course, she bragged about the attention she'd been getting in that car from day one.

"Yeah, I bet it was from some of Black's friends still trying to sniff around, huh?" David assumed.

"Ba-bee…they can sniff all they want, but they ain't got nothin over here. Especially being a friend of Black's," she replied, twisting her lips, in disgust. Immediately after her little comment, someone tooted their horn at the little hottie driving that 1966 Mustang, and she tooted back; waving, with a big grin on her face—flirting.

"Happens all the time," she bragged, driving with both hands on the wheel.
As Martie pulled into the driveway leading to David's apartment, she asked if he had left the A/C on. He didn't, and it felt like a like a sauna—hot and stuffy. Martie fanned as her skin moistened from the heat,

"You should have left the air on, or you could have left me your key. I could have checked on the place while you were gone, but you act like I was gonna come over here and dig all through your lil stuff or something," Martie said, sarcastically.

"And that's exactly what you would've done, which is why you don't have a key," David laughed. There were three messages on the answering machine, but David hesitated to check them. Ara was the only one who would leave raunchy messages, which was no biggie, but just in case

Rosalind had left a message, which was something Martie didn't need to know, David avoided checking the messages. Martie stood in front of the air conditioner, keeping cool while David went through one of his bags for the Dion Sanders jersey he bought for Junior. The blinking numbers on the answering machine got the best of Martie's nosiness. She walked over to press play.

"Aay lil woman! That's private!" David said as he darted towards the answering machine, but Martie had already pushed play.

Sydney's rusty voice requested, "David, please return my call as soon as you get this message." As Sydney was hanging up, the voicemail recorded her unintended message, saying, "This is some bull—t."

"That reminds me, what's going on with you two?" Martie asked.
David reminded Martie about what happened that night at the party and was following up with what happened with Aaron when the phone rang.

"Don't answer that!" David said, thinking it was Sydney.
When the voicemail picked up, Piggy's voice cracked, saying his name, "Da-Da—"
David snatched the receiver, "Hey boo!" he spoke.
As Martie watched David listening to whatever Piggy was telling him, it made David's eyes look hollow,

and the blood looked as if it had completely drained
from his face.